NACHIKETA

NACHIKETA

Santanu Kumar Acharya

Translated by

Ashok Mohanty

BLACK EAGLE BOOKS
Dublin, USA | Bhubaneswar, India

 Black Eagle Books
USA address:
7464 Wisdom Lane
Dublin, OH 43016

India address:
E/312, Trident Galaxy, Kalinga Nagar,
Bhubaneswar-751003, Odisha, India

E-mail: info@blackeaglebooks.org
Website: www.blackeaglebooks.org

First International Edition Published by
Black Eagle Books, 2024

NACHIKETA
by **Santanu Kumar Acharya**

Translated by **Ashok Mohanty**

Original Copyright © Santanu Kumar Acharya
Translation Copyright © Ashok Mohanty

Cover & Interior Design: Ezy's Publication

ISBN- 978-1-64560-347-4 (Paperback)
Library of Congress Control Number: 2024943078

Printed in the United States of America

ONE

Who's there?

He sat up on the bed. He rubbed his eyes and called out again – who's there?

But there was no answer from outside.

Bibhuprasad got out of bed. Should he light the lamp? But he dismissed the idea from his head thinking of something else. His ears were alert though – for any sound from outside.

A fairly quiet and calm night.

But where did the sound of those footsteps vanish? Someone had surely come and even perhaps called him by name – Bibhu! Bibhu!

Bibhuprasad opened the door. The chill wind of the dawn brought in its wake a bit of cold, some shivers and fragrances! A dawn in November.

A fabulous fragrance! Kathachampa and Muchukunda flowers were perhaps in full bloom in the garden of the landlord.

But was it the time for those flowers to bloom …?

Bibhuprasad yawned and looked around. He closed the door and went back to bed. He lifted the bed sheet from the bed and covered himself. His eyes began to close.

But his ears remained alert.

The thin whistle of a black bird could be heard from outside. A cock crowed from a distance and fell quiet. A mosquito buzzed around his face. The mosquito flew away after a while.

And after that –

He could hear a shrill whistle.

It was the whistle of a motorboat on River Mahanadi. Then he heard the sound of a train engine. The engine seemed to be moving on the bridge over Mahanadi or Kathjodi. It was perhaps Mahanadi.

Yes, yes … it was Mahanadi!

Mahanadi … a stream of water surrounded by fog … a tract of sand in a desert for the two tiny feet … the cold breeze and freezing water … the dew falling in drops … snappy wind and the tiny waves in the water … the hills and dense forests of Damapada on the other side …a green horizon … numerous pillars of gold inside the water …the sun was rising, the sun!

And after that?

Oh! After that….

He was returning … there were miles of sand behind him. And here it was; the gate of the school ahead of him!

Here, he composed songs standing near the eucalyptus tree that was kissing the skies ….

I'll kiss the skies seeking light

Spreading fragrance in every leaf …

And a little further … a small, obscure creeper … running at the feet of the eucalyptus tree … in the dust … laden with flowers …. Ungainly flowers ….

I'm the desert creeper in these sand dunes

I shall hold this earth in my lap

My thin frame shall be reinvigorated

Nectar shall flow from my sea of tears.

And here – a student stood under the small arch of that entrance – he was in Class Seven. This was a minor school in that small, alien village.

Bibhuprasad had kept staring – underneath the bed sheet, and seeing – childhood standing at a distance inside a dirty shirt and small pant; but a smile danced on the face – like a sunrise on the Mahanadi.

Footsteps could be heard again outside. Bibhuprasad again called out – who's there? But there was still no answer.

Now childhood stepped inside. Then it stopped in its tracks and looked back. Something seemed to have been left behind near the gate of the school. Childhood took stock of the situation. A marble tablet. Must have been the brainchild of a headmaster in the distant past – just that one line -

"Whatever man has done, man may do!"

It was at the same school. His father served here for the last several years and was still serving. And he studied here one day. A small boy under the small arch of the small gate of the small school of the small village. He stood … the lake slept to his right – the quiet, grave Anshupa. And the river ran to his left – the restless, yawning Mahanadi with a rocky bed! Marks of footsteps on its sandy bed … those of tigers and human beings….

He was not aware of it. Tears had rolled down from his eyes for some time; but he was not crying. He was not the type to cry. Why? It will be morning in a while. He would have his bath. Then he would spruce himself up and go out with the file of the research scholar in hand. Here it was! The key was lying below the pillow – the key of the laborartory.

* ** *

But it was morning which called out in its frosty and dewy voice. And it was calling out that day too – as abruptly as ever – Bibhu! Bibhu!

But where had it been lost all these days? Where had it floated away – like the tune of a wayward flute?

Light entered slowly through the openings in the doors and windows as if it was being strained.

Bibhuprasad got up. The memory of the fragrance of coffee from the south Indian hotel excited him. The door opened. There was indeed a dense fog outside. And an elderly man emerged out of that dense fog.

Father!

Bibhuprasad walked to him and paid his respects. Then he gulped and said, "It's indeed strange! I was dreaming of you a little while ago. And you've really come."

"I knew. I came because of that …."

"You knew? What do you mean? Were you dreaming too?"

"No, son! I know you don't have any money. It's the end of the month after all …."

Bibhuprasad looked sad; but there was an inner happiness too. He felt as if he was back in the old days. He had passed the middle school examination and come to the town – for the first time. He had enrolled himself again in the biggest school in the town. The same hostel and the same room … room number nine … his father had arrived on a similar morning … in the Talcher train.

And he would return too – on the early morning train the next day. He would not be able to sleep that night at all. The whistle of the motorboat and the sound and whistle of that train engine on the bridge would force him to wail throughout the night.

Father! Father … he would get up in a fright and call

out. He was twelve years old at the time. His roommates would take a dig at him – 'Homesick, eunuch'.

But see! His father reached him some days as if he could hear him call – on mornings like this. He banged on the door, woke him up and said, "Come on! Get up, run – run every day in the morning after you get up! Put some life into yourself! Be a sportsman. I want to see you in the State Olympics this year. Come on!"

That was the man. He was always like that. He was just a teacher in a minor school. But what about him?

No … no longer did he study in the school. A research scholarship of a hundred rupees a month was all that he got. He was a research scholar!

And what about the man who stood before him? He got thirty five rupees a month. That was all that he had been getting for the past twenty five years and he would perhaps continue to draw the same amount for ever. But look at his face!

The sun was about to rise. The fog was disappearing gradually.

Father and son kept on walking together –

"Learn to walk fast!" his father said as always, "Why are you walking like a hunchback? Look at me! Always walk like this – like a military man! Don't forget that there was a military man among your ancestors. And that was your grandfather … why do you think he had chosen me as a son-in-law …? Because I was an engineer who had returned from war and was an employee of a corporation? I didn't have anything that I could call my own – I only had agility in my feet and loads of courage in my heart. I crossed the sea of life with only these. Even when I had to carry three children on my shoulders that had lost their mother … learn to walk … learn to walk, son …!"

They had been walking towards the coffee shop.

The father walked in the front. The son followed him. More than one half of the head of one was visible behind the head of the other. Perhaps a great deal more of the back of the head should have been visible. But the boy always had his face to the ground. He had got into the habit of walking with a downcast face. He looked sad. He was turning darker by the day. What had happened to him? He was not always like this! He was so clever and quick ... a boy who used to move around swiftly humming like a bee all the time ....

His father turned around to look behind him. He stopped for a while so the person behind him would be able to catch up with him. He looked sideways ... this was his child. He looked at his hunched back! The throat was getting thinner by the day. Two veins protruded from the base of the neck and it seemed as if they lent support to his heavy head to keep it in place ... those veins!

His father had been repeatedly staring at Bibhuprasad's head. He had been thinking – the boy had such a handsome head once upon a time – of course, it was not entirely round and the right side of the skull was slightly higher! And who was responsible for this? Of course, his mother was responsible for this! In stead of putting the head of the newborn child on a soft pillow, she always kept it on her bony chest. And the result was that the child's head had been pushed inside slightly on one side. But the head had been covered with a lot of hair ... they fell in a curl on that sweet face ... but what had happened to that head and those locks of hair?

Bibhu's father walked – with his hand resting on the son's shoulder – as if he was his friend ... as if he was his younger brother.

They passed through a narrow street to emerge on the main road. This was the College Square. Bibhu's father had been staring ... towards that old College Square. Nothing new there. The same shops and the same people.

Bibhuprasad too had been staring – this was the college! Where his father had been studying I.A. or F.A. forty years ago! The college was of course not at this place earlier. It was in that school from where he himself had passed his matriculation. He also knew that his father had failed the F.A. examination from that place while he himself had passed matriculation in the first division – from that same institution. Was that all the difference between that distant 1919 and today?

But it seemed as if the reactions of the past half a century had not left any impressions on this man. Bibhuprasad had been walking alongside his father. He had been staring at his father's face and his father had been staring at the son's face.

Bibhuprasad had been staring ....

Look! He had been walking straight as a ramrod. Not a single hair had turned grey on that head. All the teeth were in place. No, it was not a lie. Those thirty two teeth blackened from years of chewing *paan* were intact inside that handsome face. Two sharp eyes had been staring from behind the straight, sharp nose on that extremely fair face!

This was his father – Sri Bhabaniprasad. Assistant Headmaster of a minor school. Oh yes, 'assistant' headmaster. Failed in F.A.! The salary was somewhere between thirty five and fifty rupees. And he had also put in about thirty five to forty years on the job – between 1920-21 and 1960-61. Of course, his service book didn't show that he had completed thirty years of service ... but the thirty years would be over soon ... very soon!

TWO

But –

This was another kind of fog. The fog of the laboratory. No, no, it was not exactly fog. This fog was not the result of the admixture of chill nightly wind of the land mass and gases originating from lukewarm bed of water. This was the fog of gases - pungent smoke – chemical 'fume'. Totally chemical. There was no trace of geography here. This was Bibhuprasad's laboratory.

Some scholar had forgotten to keep the crucible inside the fume cupboard. Fume cupboard. That was a smoke box. Pungent acidic smoke from the crucible rose at a fast pace. The ammonia bottle had perhaps been left open nearby. The strange world of dreams had been created because of the admixture of ammonia and acid – the world of dreams of a scientist.

There was a wall of glass on all sides. Coloured bottles all around. Everything seemed to be made of glass. Everything glazed. A mirage of snow covered with clouds. The echo of a flowing spring. The tap was left open. Water flowed noisily down the sink. The chemical stream was flowing down the drain of the laboratory. And after that …?

Bibhuprasad broke into a coughing fit. But he had no ears for the sound he made. He stood near the table where he was supposed to work. He had a test tube and a cleaning brush in his hand. Besides, several dirty glass containers had gathered on his table. Those had to be cleaned with soda. Work left over from yesterday. Irritating; but he was used to it.

There were numerous flies on the nearby table. Some spirit was perhaps spilled there – rectified spirit or alcohol. Large, blue flies had converged there from everywhere. Large flies greedy of fruits. But there was no fruit. Only the fragrance. Ah, the poor flies! There was no dearth of mirages even for them in this creation.

Bibhuprasad leaned forward. He held the dirty test tube under the tap. He shoved the brush inside the tube a few more times. Then he became even more active. He could hear the sound of familiar shoes from the other side of the verandah.

The professor had arrived!

He ran to Manmohan's table leaving the half-cleaned test tube behind. Smoke rose from that table. Manmohan had gone somewhere leaving the crucible on the burner. Of course, he had cautioned Bibhuprasad before leaving –

"Look! It's time for the professor to visit. I'll be back in a while; but make sure that the crucible is placed inside the fume cupboard before the professor's arrival. The old man will eat me alive if he finds this place full of smoke."

Bibhuprasad ran. The flies flew away making a humming noise. Bibhuprasad got lost amid the smoke – for a moment. The crucible was moved inside the cupboard in a flash. There was less smoke now. He ran to switch the tap off. The source of the spring vanished in no time. He looked for the ammonia bottle and put the lid on it.

"All right!" Bibhuprasad said to himself, "The world of dreams is gone now – let it go. And after that? Oh! Flies! The old man is always irritated by the flies."

Then he ran again to Manmohan's table. The spirit

bottle had actually been left open there. The flies rose to surround Bibhuprasad. He came out with one hand warding off the flies.

Bibhuprasad moved around the laboratory. Everything was tip-top! The old man liked everything to be tip-top!

Bibhuprasad's ears were alert. The sound of the shoes had been lost midway. The old man had perhaps been observing something. Perhaps some new thought had struck him – some 'idea'. The feet had stopped midway.

The old man's room was on the other side of the laboratory. There was another door to that room of course; but the old man preferred to go inside his room through the laboratory. Sometimes he entered the laboratory through another door too. At times, he entered the laboratory quietly – making sure that his shoes didn't make a sound. Sometimes he stood behind the scholars who were at work and observed them. A man lost in his own world – "Hiranyaka – the cunning rat".

A thin and short man. Supple like a cane and cruel too. The face laced with a smile and grief at the same time. Slightly large front teeth. But the old man was always in a hurry to hide those slightly large teeth when he blew a fuse rather than raising the hood and teeth like a snake – inside his thin lips. But alas! He did not succeed at it.

When he looked at the thin physique and enraged face of the old man, Bibhuprasad always recited – 'Small men have no pity.' But it didn't matter. Another phrase came to his lips soon after to counter the phrase. Looking at that face of the old man which seemed to be smiling and weeping at the same time, Bibhuprasad paid his respects silently – 'A toothy man is seldom a fool.' Not just that. Bibhuprasad was also swayed by that forehead that was getting more and more lustrous and broadened by the day. Observing the lonesome light reflecting from the shining skin of the head of the old man, Bibhuprasad said, "There's light inside that." Manmohan said, "Yes. It's true that there is light inside it. But that light is the light of the witch – it collects light during the day and emits it during the night … phosphorescent light!" Natabar said, "Yes. That light is the light of the jewel – but that jewel is the jewel of the greatly self-doubting python! It's not the Kohinoor." And so, forth the discussion continued on the light.

But all said and done, the man didn't have anything that could be called a cheek and for that reason alone, the ordinary nose on his face seemed so sharp and gorgeous to the uninitiated eye. However, Bibhuprasad always wondered about those two cheeks. When had they vanished from their resting places? Were they ever there? Were they likely to return? He had heard that they had apparently built a nest for a few days on the bare cheek bones of the old man some twelve years ago. But they flew away before laying any eggs. They flew away never to return again.

This old professor!

Bibhuprasad was busy with his work with his back to the door as if he had not seen him. He was busy with his teeth clenched and eyes dilated. The work was extremely easy. Bibhuprasad loosened the screw on one of the clamps. It was not as if there was any need to wrestle with the clamp to accomplish it. But there was a need for that – like that sincere word 'and' used so often by the old man. Needless to say, that word 'and' was extremely powerful and active!

Bibhuprasad carefully listened to what the old man had to say at the commencement of a task – that sincere and powerful word 'and' hit him again. "There's just one thing to remember – sincerity 'and' sense of duty." Bibhuprasad smiled. The sound of the old man's shoes melted away behind the back door of the laboratory. The old man entered his chamber. Bibhuprasad slumped into a chair, relaxed.

Every scholar had his own technique to appease the old man. Take the case of a research scholar, Manmohan, for instance, who worked in this laboratory. Over there – on that seat. Manmohan was from a rich family. His father was a high-ranking officer. He was stinking rich; but Manmohan wore a tattered, terylene Hawaiian to the laboratory (he himself called it 'terykhaddar') and an old, dirty shark-skin trouser (which he called shark-bark or iguana's skin). Similarly, a pair of 'dead' shoes also formed part of his laboratory outfit. All these were supposed to be evidence of his poverty. Manmohan exploited the sentiments of the old man. The old man had a soft corner for poverty and he was aware of it.

Similarly, the scholar named Natabar also had his own method. He was actually poor; but the creature was an unfortunate poor and his face was the prime reason for all his misfortunes! His face was the cause of several misfortunes like an inauspicious piece of diamond! One was not a king and yet there were all the signs of a king written on his forehead! Natabar shaved his head at intervals and hit his face with his own fists at times. His specialty was to scratch his face with a blunt razor to leave marks all over. If anyone could really claim to have the old man under his influence, it was Natabar; 'Natia – the Rascal' was his nickname.

Bibhuprasad sat beside a table – on a high stool. A bunch of cassia fruits lay on the table. Bibhuprasad cut them into pieces with a knife. A sweet fragrance was in the air.

He separated the seeds from the fruits. He was perhaps not sure as yet which part of the fruits would be useful. The covering of the fruits or the seeds? But that was one of his important jobs that day.

Days passed in this manner in the laboratory. It was like an indolent girl absentmindedly pricking her soft finger with a needle while stitching a garland and falling asleep – falling asleep for years on end – Bibhuprasad perhaps fell asleep on the high stool of the laboratory in a similar manner – especially on some days like this one.

Manmohan rushed in like an eagle. With a bundle of papers in his hand. Dumping the bundle on the table, he slumped into a chair, looking exhausted. He turned the discoloured table fan towards him selfishly and gasped for breath.

Bibhuprasad continued to peel the cassia seeds. He picked up a seed now and then and sniffed at it for some inexplicable reason. As he tried to straighten his creased nose and eyebrows, he picked up another cassia seed to press it to his nose without being aware of it.

Manmohan's eyes were closing as he enjoyed the breeze; but there was a faint smile on his lips. He seemed to be dreaming. Perhaps he kept smiling, noticing the bewildered face of Bibhuprasad sniffing at the cassia seeds. He seemed to be biding his time to make a comment. Perhaps nothing suitable struck him at the moment. Hence, he lay in wait.

Bibhuprasad took yet another seed to his nose.

Manmohan could not take it any longer. It was as if some vulgar scene had tickled him. He came out of his reverie. He said in a loud voice, "Hey! Why are you sniffing at those seeds like that? I'm going out of my mind. Stop it! That rascal Natia said he sniffed at that Ramanna's wife the same way. You too belong to the same species …? What kind of animals are you people?"

Bibhuprasad stared, looking amazed. What was he sniffing indeed? Manmohan's lips, singed with smoking too many cigarettes, were curled. Manmohan put on such airs before making a personal attack on someone else. He turned grave like still water under which the crocodiles waited for their prey. But the water had already turned muddy without his knowledge.

Bibhuprasad was on his guard. He knew Manmohan was about to launch into a vicious attack. He kept looking at Manmohan's face and eyes as he prepared his self-defense.

Manmohan was not really all that handsome; but he had a good frame. He was quite tall, healthy and smooth in complexion. He was neither fair nor dark. Somewhat grayish-brown. He had a good head of hair. He often looked from the corners of his eyes but he was not cockeyed. His eyes were large but not intelligent. Slightly foxy, cunning and clever but mysterious. It was difficult to fathom the language of those eyes. It could not be predicted when those eyes would call the grapes sour or sweet. Thus, he knew how to move with the times. Such eyes were in great demand in this age.

Looking at Manmohan, Bibhuprasad said, "Do you know? Natabar is no longer obsessed with the fragrance of the body of Ramanna's wife. He is now possessed with the fragrance of some kind of blue lily and Kathachampa flower! You know that?"

"What bloody blue lily and Kathachampa?" Manmohan again seemed to come out of a reverie and said, "But she was your dish … have you started exchanging each other's dish?" Then he laughed and said, "Do you know? I'm regularly seeing your dish these days. She is to be seen here almost everyday! What's cooking?"

Bibhuprasad had been waiting just for this one. He

became grave all of a sudden and swelled like a porcupine with its quills sticking out. But he relented like any other day and to cajole those swollen up quills into sleep was another specialty of Manmohan.

Bibhuprasad remained quiet. And it was as if Manmohan's job was to shut everyone up – in this laboratory!

But none of these was a personal trait of Manmohan. He had inherited all these from his father. His ancestors were Manmohan's best identity – they were all government servants for generations. The other day, he claimed that one of his ancestors even served the East India Company. Apart from this, his family had a glorious past. They had earned fame as patrons of education since his grandfather's time. His grandfather was an efficient bureaucrat in the estate department between 1865 and 1878 when Ravenshaw Sahib was the Commissioner of Orissa and Superintendent of the Tributary Estate of Cuttack. And he had become the right hand man of Ravenshaw Sahib in due course. The infamous Na'Anka Famine occurred during his tenure in 1866. Apart from that, Manmohan claimed that his ancestors had turned into distinguished Oriyas of the time in the process of distributing relief in the most terrible floods of the century in 1866-67. Manmohan was the descendant of this eminent family. This proven claim on Orissa was the real identity of Manmohan.

Manmohan started taking a dig at Bibhuprasad when he found him subdued and quiet. He batted those foxy eyelids and said, "Do you know what Natabar has done in the meantime? What do you think he has started now? A new paper!"

"New paper?" Bibhuprasad had still not let his guards down. He knew Manmohan very well. Manmohan was a Japanese wrestler. He didn't use his muscles to wrestle – he did so with his fingertips. He had been trained from childhood to poke his fingertips on the vulnerable areas of his opponent's body to immobilize him. Manmohan was a townee. He didn't play games by the rule book like Natabar and Bibhuprasad who were basically village lads. He was adept at playing tactical games. Using one such tactic, Manmohan said, "You know something? Natabar is cornered now. The professor knows that he is married!"

"Married? Who? Natabar?" Bibhuprasad was amazed indeed.

Bibhuprasad looked at Natabar's empty seat and for some reason he looked somewhat uncertain. Natabar indeed looked terribly absentminded for the past few days. He also looked as if he was unwell.

Bibhuprasad was apprehensive though Natabar's falling health was not his biggest concern. He was worried about the professor's anger. The professor would definitely get angry – especially if he came to know that anyone from this laboratory even thought of marriage – this was known to everyone. Manmohan's cooked-up news seemed to be a bad omen for the laboratory, thought Bibhuprasad.

Glancing at Natabar's empty seat, Bibhuprasad again saw those green flies. They kept flying – as they were flying from the beginning.

Yes, he was Natabar – Manmohan's enemy from the previous birth.

But he was Natabar whose identity comprised a number of strange words. Like Ramanna's wife... Malli Apa... camel hair cap... Ola Rauta alias Lord William Bentick... etc., etc. A number of strange and worrying words. And, that god-given look and that artificial, bald head along with all these – Natabar created himself from the conflict between these two – unintelligible Natabar!

But it was not as if this shaven head of Natabar was only something to appease the professor – a charm or a hypnotic amulet or some such tantric arrangement like the 'terykhaddar' of Manmohan or the scholarly, sad face of Bibhuprasad. It has been said from the beginning that Natabar was a solid diamond – the symbol of an unknown infallibility and a precursor of a storm – a huge diamond like a flash of lightning.

The history of Natabar's shaven head was like this – the shaven head started the year his father expired – he had passed the matriculation examination that year in high second division. He had missed the first division narrowly. A thunderbolt hit that head suddenly. His father died of some terrible disease and Natabar had to shave his head leaving only a few strands of hair to show that he had lost a parent. Like a few strands of hair flying from a coconut tree that had been hit by a thunderbolt.

Natabar had just taken admission in the college. He knew what a college was even though he had come from the mofussil, and he also knew the position of a rustic with a pigtail at that place. College – the place where the physical beauty of young men and women was displayed through their tresses – like the silk cocoon of the larvae which was about to metamorphose into a butterfly.

While leaving the village, Natabar had scrounged through her mother's box and discovered the thing which he had longed to possess throughout his life. But who knew that he had discovered the root of all disasters of his life that day – from inside the box of his widowed mother.

It was a cap! Made from the hair of a camel, sheep or some other strange animal. The hair had come off at a few places. Still, it was a magnificent, shining, black and white cap. That invaluable property discovered in his mother's box actually belonged to his father. Part of the history of his family…. But let it go, it would come later.

Natabar hid the cap inside his small tin suitcase after stealing it from his mother's box. He spread a piece of paper on it to hide it from view. But he was not aware of the fact that his mother had sometime left a packet of *chuda* on that piece of paper for his foreign-bound son – inside the suitcase!

Natabar reached Cuttack. Ramanna, who belonged to his village, worked as a peon at the Collectorate. It had been arranged that Natabar would stay in his house. It was also decided that he didn't have to pay any house rent if he looked after the studies of Ramanna's three children for an hour or two every day. Apart from that, rice, dal and other things would come from the village. Natabar became a guest at Ramanna's place – after all these agreements were made.

He had to go to the college next day. Natabar opened his tin box. He discovered the packet of *chuda* tied in a piece of dirty cloth immediately upon opening the box.

The packet of *chuda!* Memento of the widowed mother. But Natabar was terribly angry. He dumped the packet outside and ran his fingers over his shaven head. Releasing a deep sigh, he waited for a while.

He recovered after a while and caressed the crumpled paper below the packet. He waited. For some unknown reason, there was a thumping inside his chest. As if he felt the necessity of looking in different directions.

Ramanna's wife was breast-feeding her baby just beyond the doorstep. A corner of the verandah had been screened with a thin flat strip of wood which served as Natabar's room. A rickshaw puller used to sleep in the nights there earlier … on a rent of three rupees per month. Natabar raised his face to stare at the thatched roof … a half-smoked country cigar was still stuck there – used by the former tenant.

Natabar moved to a corner – caressing the smooth hair of the cap, he placed it on his head. The cap fit his head perfectly. His father's cap. Natabar longed for a mirror. But alas! He had forgotten to carry a mirror with him. But he could perhaps see his prince-like face without the help of a mirror as he caressed the cap on his head.

Prince?

Natabar felt elated. He caressed his face and the cap on his head time and again.   Royal! Everything seemed to be royal!

Natabar started college all of a sudden. He took one step ahead. Then he thought of something and retraced his step. He removed the cap from his head, quietly put it inside his shirt and walked down the steps to go to college.

Ramanna's wife had stared. The baby had dropped off to sleep on her chest. The children had left for school. Ramanna had also left for the court.

Natabar was walking briskly out of the house. Suddenly, Ramanna's wife called him, "What are you hiding inside your shirt, Nata?"

Natabar was startled. So Ramanna's wife had also eyed his cap. Natabar stopped in his tracks.

Ramanna's wife placed the baby on a swing hanging from the ceiling and picked up the *paan*-box.

Nata said, "Why, Bhauja, it's nothing. It's only a notebook."

But Ramanna's wife could not be dismissed so easily. It was not easy to avoid her cunning eyes.

She smiled slightly and put a *paan* inside her mouth

before saying, "Come on! Something large seems to be hidden inside your shirt – and you say that it's a notebook!"

Then she thought of something and said smilingly, "Why should this guy hide himself in so many clothes being a man … why don't you show it – what are you hiding inside that shirt?"

Natabar's face coloured. It was already time for the college, and there was this sudden attack by Ramanna's wife. The cap felt uncomfortable beneath his shirt, but Natabar could not muster enough courage. His head, unused to a cap, started reeling. He blushed profusely.

But the curiosity of Ramanna's wife was not to be satiated with that. It didn't take her even a moment to infuse Natabar with a bit of juice to lift his spirits.

Natabar's hair stood on their ends when Ramanna's wife pulled out the cap from inside his shirt and ran her thin and beautiful fingers on the smooth fur of the cap.

"What a beautiful cap! Where did you find this, Nata? Does it belong to your father? Looks like a cap worn in the jatras!" Ramanna's wife placed the cap on Natabar's head as she said this and bowing a bit like an onlooker with admiring eyes, said, "Oh no! Why did God have to place this prince in the house of a poor man! Poor orphan … only if the father were alive … he would have been proud of his son … how could the mother bear the pangs of separation after sending the son away from her …."

Natabar got a bit more panicky when he saw his own reflection in the mirror of Ramanna's wife's eyes. However, much he tried, he could no longer see the person behind the glass of the mirror. Gradually, Ramanna's wife stood before Natabar as a mysterious character and the woman continued to remain mysterious for him for all time to come.

Natabar turned his face towards the college.

Ramanna's wife was left behind. A question mark. The cap was on his head – the symbol of a prince – the symbol of self-esteem.

But that symbol of self-esteem – like all other symbols of false dignity - became the cause of serious economic disaster for Natabar.

The cap that Ramanna's wife had placed on his head didn't come off Natabar's head again. The cap was on his head all the time, whether he was in the college or sleeping on his bed. There was a change in his attire in two months time. The half pant and half shirt lengthened to turn into full pant and full shirt. Natabar smiled when his widowed mother wrote from the village, "Son, be careful at that expensive place." He said to himself, "Look at this. Mothers of other boys caution them to be wary of the traffic in the city. And my mother asks me to be careful of the expensive place! Ha!"

Natabar bought chocolates and sweets for Ramanna's children now and then. Proffering a packet to Ramanna's wife, he said, "Take this, Bhauja. My gift for the Puja!"

Ramanna's wife would smile and say, "I wish you would make a present like this to your widowed mother and say, 'Take this, mother! Taste it …!'"

Natabar looked crestfallen. Still, he would force a smile on his lips and say, "There is nothing to taste in this packet. There is fragrance here … the fragrance of blue lily and the Kathachampa!"

But the princely state of Natabar didn't continue much longer. The meeting of the free studentship board was scheduled in a few days. Natabar applied for free studentship.

Natabar's hair was still short by the time the board met. There was a pigtail beside that! That had to be hidden too. When his name was called for the interview, one of his classmates shouted from behind, "Listen, you idiot. Remove that cap before going in. Otherwise, you'd have to forget about the free studentship. Do you have any idea how much that cap costs?"

Natabar looked back. It was Asfar Mian, the son of the tobacconist. He too had come to attend the interview. Natabar knew Asfar Mian came to the college on his motorbike. But that day he looked different. The rich guy Asfar stood before the interview board today in the garb of a fakir with a begging bowl in hand.

Asfar shouted again, "Hey idiot! That cap costs a hundred bucks, do you know that? You've come to meet the board with a hundred-rupee cap on your head! Do you know who is on that board?"

But Natabar had no time for Asfar. Instead of removing the cap and putting it in his pocket, he barged into the chamber. Three fat professors sat inside.

"You are Natabar Raut?" asked the professor sitting in the middle with a smile on his face.

"Yes, Sir, I'm Natabar Raut," Natabar answered as he gulped.

"Okay." The three professors discussed something in a low-pitched voice and broke into laughter.

Natabar stood ramrod straight – like a prince.

"Okay," one of them stopped laughing and asked, "Are you related to Mr. Raut?"

"Which Mr. Raut, Sir?' Natabar Raut, son of Ola Raut, had stared at the triumvirate, perplexed.

"Don't you know Mr. Raut? He is the D.M. How are you related to him?"

"D.M. District Magistrate? How am I related to him?" Natabar felt like breaking into a sob. He started sobbing and said, "Sir, I'm a poor student. I come from the mofussil. My father's name is Ola Raut. He expired six months back. I'm in no way related to the D.M., Sir."

"Your father's name is Ola Raut?" someone asked again.

"Yes, Sir," Natabar answered quickly.

"Ola or William?" the interviewer asked and laughed.

Natabar felt a searing pain in his chest. He ran his fingers on his forehead without being aware of it. His fingers touched a deep mark above the left eye.

That mark was there from his childhood. The day his father had thrown a sharp instrument at him – from that day.

That day his father had been sewing a mat just outside the house when he returned from school. Natabar watched his father standing nearby. His father had shaved off most of the long lock of hair on his head and tied the rest in a pigtail.

Natabar watched his father at work for a while. Then he pushed closer to him, and staring at him in the face, asked, "Father! Is your name really Ola Raut?"

Stopping in his tracks, his father stared hard at his son's face.

The kid had not been able to observe the expression on his father's face.

He bubbled with enthusiasm and said, "Father! Perhaps your real name is Lord William Bentick. People are mistaken and they have distorted your name. We were taught about Lord William Bentick in school today. Here, look at his picture. He looks exactly like you."

Ola Raut had continued to glare at his son's face.

Natabar was encouraged by the silence. He said, "Father! You remember how you had saved Baurani, mother of that Gurubaria? Did you not save her from drowning? Similarly, Lord William Bentick had abolished the system of Sati and saved our country ...."

But the child never got a chance to complete the sentence. A sharp instrument hit him on the forehead out of the blue. The child fell at that spot in a heap.

Natabar stood before the free studentship board quietly, running his fingers on his head. Finally, he was told by the board, "Listen. You cannot cheat us! There is no doubt that you are the son of a zamindar. Your looks and this cap ... do you think we are all fools sitting here? Do you think you can take us for a ride so easily?"

"No, Sir," Natabar started to argue. "I am not at all the son of a rich man. I am the son of a poor farmer. There is only my widowed mother at home. I've got a high second division. I won't be able to continue with my studies if I don't get a free studentship. I'll be ruined, Sir."

A grey-headed member advised Natabar, "We were not getting enough food to eat during our childhood. But now you people wear hundred-rupee caps on your heads and still apply for free studentship. And, on top of that, you break into a sob and claim that you are poor. What about us in that case? We still don't get enough to eat even after becoming professors. How would we introduce our children?"

Natabar failed to get free studentship. It was not just that. It became common knowledge that he came from a very rich family and was related to many aristocratic people in the city. Hence, he would never ever be eligible to get free studentship.

Natabar thought he would have to say good bye to studies that day. He could only somehow manage to deposit his fees in the college because of the help of Ramanna's wife. That day he went to the banks of Mahanadi too. The cap made of camel hair was in his hand.

He hurled the cap all of a sudden into the swelling river and said to himself, "Bloody Ola Raut! Can his son ever become Lord William Bentick? The son of the father with a pigtail!"

He hit his face a few times with his fist. He returned home in a low spirit. From that day, he started giving tuition to other students. Independent business!

But that did not mean Natabar was through with his anger with the cap. He had decided that he would go to the village that year during the Dussehra vacation and release all his pent-up anger by taking it out on his widowed mother. Natabar started shaving his head from that day. That was perhaps a solemn oath taken by him.

They talked to each other when they went for coffee after taking an hour and half's break from the laboratory work – about their families, their secrets, love affairs, conflicts, research, politics and whatever else that came to mind. And this was also the most appropriate time when even the onlooker Bibhuprasad introduced himself to others. But he was also properly introduced to someone else at this time – and that was, Bibhuprasad himself.

The journey started from the verandah of the laboratory. Manmohan inside his 'terykhaddar', Natabar with his wagging pigtail and Bibhuprasad amid the 'wealth' of his famine-stricken outward cover. The three gentle boys came out in a procession. They crossed the first hurdle quietly on tiptoes – the professor's chamber. They peeped inside through the opening of the door. The old man was immersed in books. Then they looked at each other and continued on their path without making the slightest noise.

Another person joined them there. A dark, thin and

clean-shaven boy. He could not of course be called a boy. He was a researcher and lecturer. No one could say how old he was. But George Barnard Shaw described one such clean-shaven homo sapien in the beginning of one of his plays and said that he could be anywhere from 18 to 80. This was Mr. Sethi.

Mr. Sethi was a married man. Father of three children. But he was not a proud father. By nature, he was not even perhaps aware of the meaning of the word 'pride'. The problem of marriage was over for him when he was studying in class nine. But family life had borne him down since that day like the bundle of clothes carried by a washer man on his back. His first child arrived from this bundle the day he was stepping inside the examination hall to appear at the matriculation examination.

He always narrated this story about himself especially when someone pointed at his weak physique and said, "Mr. Sethi! Drink some milk every day as a matter of habit – let's see if that brings about some improvement in you!"

Mr. Sethi replied smilingly, "Hey! You're talking about drinking milk. But do I have any such luck! And the person who should have provided for me has snatched it away from me."

In order to explain the matter clearly, Mr. Sethi started in a good-humored manner – "I had secured the highest mark in English in my matriculation examination narrating about my experiences about drinking milk in an essay. And you must have known that I had stood first in the matriculation examination that year – I had that distinction only by narrating my experiences with drinking milk. Would you like to hear about that?"

They were near the college library at the time. A few girls were passing by. For the benefit of their ears and to have some fun, Mr. Sethi shouted, "Hey! Take this telegram!"

A few girls actually turned around to look but they walked away smiling upon seeing Mr. Sethi.

Mr. Sethi laughed and said, "The school clerk called from behind – 'Take your telegram. Hey Sethi! There's news for you! Give us sweets! You have a son! A son!'

"I was about to get inside the examination hall at the time. There were a thousand people around me – examinees and their parents.

"I had once insulted this person because he had tried to keep a part of my scholarship money for himself. So, this was his vengeance. It was a telegram indeed! I started howling. I was surrounded by all the students. The ink pot in my hand had shaken and my clothes were a sight.

"The clerk was smiling. He said, 'Hey! Are you mad or what? A son is born to you … this is good news! You're crying as if your father is dead.'"

Manmohan laughed – a sarcastic laugh. He said, "A man can indeed put up with the news of his father's death; but such a bad news, that too just before the examination! Do you know? My grandmother was also pregnant when my younger sister was born. My mother was so ashamed of herself that she asked grandmother to go for an abortion. She was already eight months gone at the time. Grandmother refused. Our relationship with our grandfather's family was severed that day."

Mr. Sethi ignored Manmohan and said, "The bell rung for the examination. The examinees went to their seats. Sethi too went to his place. The question paper for English was distributed. Sethi looked at the paper; but nothing was visible to him. He could only hear one sound – a newborn baby crying …. Perhaps that sound didn't come from anyone else. It was the lamentation of the desires and high expectations sealed inside Sethi's chest.

"Suddenly, he saw a question – Write an essay on any of the following topics:

(a)   Life of a village washer man
(b)   If you were the Jamsaheb of Nawanagar
(c)   Your pet dog
(d)   Your enemy

"Suddenly, Sethi attacked the (d) portion of the question with the sword of a violent pen. He started, 'As I write this essay on them with this pen, they are rushing towards me in the garb of Duryodhan and Dushasan … they are my children. It would be my duty to annihilate this Kaurav dynasty. It would be my bounden duty to get this dynasty of Yadu drunk to the brim with Kadambari and help them destroy themselves ….'"

"Bravo, bravo … fantastic! This is the theory of birth control!" Manmohan patted Mr. Sethi on the back and said, "But had this theory of yours gained so much of popularity at that time that you secured the highest mark in English?"

Natabar was quiet until then. Suddenly, he answered Manmohan's question and said, "It's true that common people in Orissa could not have appreciated such destructive attitude at that time. But there were intellectuals … especially professors in English or the dogs that licked their boots – who would have been taken in by the idea! Their hands would have itched to award marks."

Manmohan stopped for a while. He glared at Natabar, the rascal.

"I don't like this farm boy for this reason. He does not know how to talk in civil society …." Manmohan considered it to be a personal attack. 'Dogs of Englishmen' – these words hurt Manmohan for some reason.

Natabar was prepared for a fight. They had not yet crossed the college quadrangle. As Bibhuprasad tried to quieten them down, Mr. Sethi finished his discourse about himself briefly.

He said, "Say, listen. Do you think my essay was only confined to that? Has anyone ever stood first by writing that bit only?"

"Why not?" Manmohan shrieked, "My uncle got I.C.S. only by writing an essay of ten lines! Another uncle of mine spoke only two words to the Police Sahib who was only too happy to offer him a job in the police force!"

"Don't give me that crap! I know your uncle. He persuaded someone to jump into the Ganges as the Police Sahib reached the spot and then jumped after him – he made out that the man was drowning and he 'rescued' him ...."

Manmohan protested, "Listen to this fellow! Is this the story about my uncle? Whose story are you telling and do you know my uncle at all? Do you mean to say that everyone on this earth is my uncle?"

Everyone burst into laughter. Natabar too understood his mistake and joined them. Bibhuprasad convulsed with laughter. Mr. Sethi was narrating the rest of his story breathlessly. No one listened to that. But Bibhuprasad had heard about his achievement many times earlier and he remembered it.

A sad incident in Mr. Sethi's life was like this –

His wife was a pampered girl of eleven when Mr. Sethi had gone to his in-laws' house for the first time after marriage. A glass of donkey's milk with cream was brought for the son-in-law (Mr. Sethi said he had no occasion to know what cow's milk was like in his childhood ... for that matter, he had never tasted any kind of milk. The simple reason was that there was neither any cow nor even a donkey in their house. For the first time, he would have tasted donkey's milk in his father-in-law's place). But alas! He didn't have the good fortune of drinking that either for his child-wife ran in and snatched the glass of milk from his hand and shrieked, "See mother! Some thief has entered our house to steal milk. Kick him out of this place …."

They returned the same way after having coffee. Ah! How refreshing this break was! Politics, arguments, hurling abuses at each other – everything ran hand in hand. Bibhuprasad left the group to be on his own for a while. It was not a new place. The same library, the same sun dial, the same portico, the same chinese box trees. The same deodar, the cawing of the crows, shrill music coming in from the radios in the shops, 'interlude' from the sitar, sweet tunes from the flute. Everything was in a jumble there. In spite of everything, it was possible to feel the lightest special touch of each of the seasons at such moments.

Standing below a high, majestic window fitted with multi-coloured glass of the semi-circular, Greek pagoda-like library, Bibhuprasad said to Natabar by the side of a dome-shaped chinese box tree, "Perhaps this is the fort of that princess! The moat … deep, muddy swamp … shhhh, don't shout … she'll wake up!"

Natabar was not a poet; but it could not be denied that he was a lively young man. He supported Bibhuprasad and said, "Sure, sure. Take a look! There is that placard on the table – 'Silence please'".

On getting adequate support, the illusory bird, just freed from laboratory fumes, flew towards the vacant silence of the skies, flapping its wings noisily and returned abruptly – like a homing pigeon. He found himself lost as he sniffed at a leaf of the chinese box tree and started dreaming, forgetting everyone else. And that divine person appeared from inside everything exactly at that time – his father! Bibhu's father – Bhabaniprasad!

Introducing his father to Natabar, Bibhuprasad said, "Father was with me the day I took admission in this college. I remember father pointing at this library and saying, 'Bibhuprasad! This is your real mother! When would you make an appearance from out of its wombs? When would you see the light of the world? And when would the world be illuminated by you?'

"'Very soon, father,' I had answered mechanically.

"But he was not happy with that. He said, 'Who knows? I don't know if I would be alive by then – to see that birthday of yours! Very difficult! Very difficult, son!'"

Natabar too slipped away all of a sudden. He could no longer climb the mountain – in step with Bibhuprasad. Now when Bibhuprasad roamed in the world of memory all by himself, he found himself somewhere else – where there was no Natabar, Manmohan, Mr. Sethi or any one else.

Bibhuprasad discovered himself –

That day he had stared at this temple of learning with tears in his eyes. What could he say in response to the last remark of his father? But he knew what his father's real fear was. It was not actually the fear of death; it was an even more painful fear.

Their small family had to prepare itself for this eventuality for four long months ever since the results of Bibhuprasad's matriculation examination were published – for his admission into the college.

Bhabaniprasad called his three children to him every day after school was over. Discussions took place about the future of the family. Bibhuprasad sat in the middle of the bed – he was the focus of discussion. His two younger brothers sat on either side of him. One of them studied in class nine or ten, and the other was in class four. They were the judges. The father led the discussion.

Discussions began. Father asked, "All right! Is it advisable to pursue studies in the science stream? What is its future? Explain it to me, son. We are only half-educated. The ultimate objective of my life was to pass M.A. and deliver nonstop, scholarly lectures in Sanskrit. But that was not to be. My father turned into an ascetic just as I was about to appear at F.A. examination."

"Why did grandpa turn into an ascetic, father? Was anyone deranged in our family?" the brother studying in class ten asked.

"No, no, no …." Bhabaniprasad shook his head vehemently and said, "Impossible! No one was deranged or diseased in our family. We were extremely rich at one time. My great grandfather said that we were zamindars before seven generations. But the Sunset Law introduced during the time of Lord Cornwallis – remember your history book in class seven? Our zamindari was auctioned off at that time. We became commoners from that time and we became teachers for seven generations after that. Our family is a family of teachers."

"But why was the zamindari auctioned? Couldn't those idiots deposit the measly taxes in time? Ah! What a bunch of stupid idlers!"

This was the comment of Bibhuprasad. Although he had heard the answer to the question time and again, Bibhuprasad raised the question repeatedly – in family deliberations of these kinds. Bibhuprasad always got terribly angry with that stupid, unenterprising ancestor. The reason was that he was gradually able to understand as a man of this world that immeasurable distance and difference between a family of teachers and a family of zamindars!

Bhabaniprasad distanced himself for some time from his children at this moment, especially from that son who had passed matriculation in the first division. It was as if he himself felt the pain inflicted on his ancestor; but that eternal smile again returned to his lips gradually. He answered confidently, "But what was his fault? You cannot blame your ancestors for your poverty. Who knows what situation prevailed then – everything depends on one's mental condition. I've heard my father saying how that 'man' of 'that' generation abdicated the zamindari and went to Puri with his wife and son before he turned into an ascetic. He renounced this world. The zamindari was auctioned off as the taxes could not be deposited in time. Who could be held guilty for that?"

"He went to Puri. That was all for the good. But why had he given birth to a son? To turn him into an ascetic too?" Bibhuprasad flared up.

But Bhabaniprasad was not in the least angry with his son's outburst. In his ever-forgiving voice, he said, "My son! We cannot say anything for certain. How can we disregard the dialectics and values of that age? How can we show such disrespect? This is history. It's not just the history of a family, son! It is the history of the thought process of an age. There is no apparent justification for people like us in favour of abdicating such a large zamindari and going to Puri with the only son. But if it is true that they had renounced the world – (and that was their firm belief – don't disbelieve their belief) – because they had a dream which justified their behaviour. If I had a dream like that today, I might as well go mad and run away from here.

Perhaps you too might act the same way. In that case …?"

Aniruddha, the youngest son, leaned closer to the lantern. Bhabaniprasad raised the wick of the lantern and said, "The old man dreamt one night that Jagannath and Balabhadra have materialized in front of their palace in the garb of Nitaigaur and are performing *kirtan*. He came out of the palace when he heard the *kirtan*. He was followed by his wife and his only son who had latched on to a corner of her mother's sari. They followed, and the two brothers, Kalia and Balia, their beloved friends and guests, led them signalling all the time to follow them. They had been beckoning …

Come … come … come … come … follow us … us …
follow … o … o … o …o … o …o
follow … o o o o …o …o …o

Bhabaniprasad's hair stood on their ends as he narrated the story of his ancestors. He was somewhat overexcited, and in trying to explain that weird crooning to the children through his own singing and acting, he started singing a few of his favourite bhajans.

Bhabaniprasad was himself a music-lover. He had tried to teach the children to sing, harmonium in hand. But it seemed that, in this new generation, that quality had been trying to fly away somewhere in gaseous form. It was perhaps his responsibility to keep it tied down.

Stopping Bhabaniprasad in the middle of his acting, Aniruddha asked all of a sudden, "Where was that palace of ours, father?"

Everyone burst into laughter. The child blushed. He hid his face inside his tiny palms.

Pulling the child to his lap and kissing him several times on his cheeks, Bhabaniprasad tried to chastise the other children –

"Be careful! Never laugh when small children ask questions. This is bad manners. They have their self-respect even though they are young. Small children lose out. You have no idea that I had lost out one day in my childhood in these circumstances. I was a kid of one and a half years when my mother expired. I grew up being breast-fed by my aunt; but the world is not a simple place. Its ways are extremely complex. My uncle was a teacher. He was a poor man. It was difficult for him to make ends meet. We didn't know what curry was. Aunty used to rub a bit of gur on our upper lips before we sat down to eat watered rice. I and my three cousins polished off a pot of watered rice each as we licked our lips. In this generation, you cannot understand the sufferings of our generation. We grew up in this manner. I returned to Cuttack from my uncle's place. Father lived at Cuttack and gave private tuition in some rich man's house. I was introduced to the alphabets when I was six years old. I passed the minor examination at fourteen and enrolled in matriculation after that."

"In which school were you studying?" asked Minaketan, the second son.

"Me?" Bhabaniprasad answered, "Why? I was studying in Pearymohan Academy, the most famous school of that time!"

"What about money? Did your father pay so much of money?" Bibhuprasad became curious all of a sudden.

"Yes … no … father was not paying the money. He was not paying … means he was in no position to pay," Bhabaniprasad faltered a bit, as on any other day, when the matter came up for discussion.

"Why? He was giving private tuition in a rich man's house, wasn't he? Weren't you saying that just now?" Minaketan argued.

"Yes, but that money was chickenfeed. Besides … of course, he couldn't be faulted for that … anyone in his age would perhaps do the same thing," said Bhabaniprasad in a tired voice.

"What's it, father," Minaketan asked again.

"What are you asking?" Bibhuprasad answered on behalf of his father. As if reprimanding his younger brother, he said, "Don't you know? You're asking this time and again. Grandpa was taking opium …."

"Opium? Our grandpa?" Aniruddha creased his nose in disgust.

"No son! Does anyone hate his ancestor in this manner? He took opium – not for intoxication – not to get bombed – but to forget himself," Bhabaniprasad patted Aniruddha on the back.

"Then why did he want to forget himself?" Minaketan butted in.

"Ah!" Bibhuprasad felt suffocated. He made everyone aware that they had digressed too far from their original topic of discussion, and in the manner of providing a finishing touch to the discussions of the evening, he said, "Listen! Grandpa took opium – because of the death of grandmother. Grandpa was only twenty five year old at the time. He could have married again had he desired so; but he didn't. But our father …! Do you know how much superior our father is compared to grandpa? We are the sons of a sincere assistant headmaster. But our father himself happens to be the son of an opium-addict, selfish and greedy man! This is the difference between our two generations …. We are marching ahead … marching ahead and we would continue to march ahead – taking giant steps – I'll study in the science stream, father … science!"

Bhabaniprasad became grave all of a sudden. Some

mysterious line appeared on his face. It was neither self-satisfaction nor sorrow. But the children got busy with their own work. Preparations for the next day's studies.

But it was not the end of discussions. That family discussion raised its head again from inside the soft sand of economics in another wonderful place.

It could not be decided in those one or two sessions whether Bibhuprasad would opt for science or arts in college. The need arose for repeated meetings in the summer vacation. Bibhu was adamant that he would study in the science stream. The reason was he had passed matriculation with distinction – in first division.

Bhabaniprasad's ideas about the science stream were not all that conservative. But a totally wrong notion had been given to him by one of the boys from his village who had failed the I.Sc. examination. As they were talking one day, the boy had cautioned Bhabaniprasad, "Brother! Be careful! If you want your son to fail the examination, admit him in the science stream. But remember. There is a hurdle called the practical examination there which is waiting for people like us. And if he flunks there, the boy will be ruined. But you'll be ruined before that. Take care!"

Such a warning put Bhabaniprasad in a great dilemma. He was worried like the mother of a girl who was about to deliver a child for the first time.

The boy continued, "Studying in the science stream is not easy, brother! This is a business and it is also meant for the children of those businessmen … the basic thing is that the father should be capable enough. It won't do only if the boy is good at studies. It would be all over if his provider falters …."

Bhabaniprasad became apprehensive. He thought to himself – yes, that was right! The horse jumped around when the post was strong; but could this post take the strain? It was not an ordinary subject that the boy would take up private tuition and see through his studies. Things were not so easy when one opted for the science stream. The boy could not take it easy even for a moment. Apart from that, the boy had to be provided with enough money for his upkeep on the first of every month – not a day could be delayed!

Bhabaniprasad broke down with this inner conflict. Several apprehensions came from several directions. He thrashed around like a fish caught in a net. At times, he got so frightened that he unnerved the children while chatting with them in the night. Quite unnecessarily, he asked that terrible but extremely realistic question –

"Suppose something happened to me during your studies? How would you complete your studies ... your younger brothers would study ... how would they get ahead in life?"

A deep black shadow suddenly descended into the room. Everyone was quiet. Aniruddha inched closer to the others – inside the family's circle.

After a while …. Bibhuprasad suddenly grabbed a large grasshopper perching on the lantern staring at the light with its large eyes, stretching its long moustaches towards him and preparing itself for the next jump. In order to step out of that black shadow, he dragged the basic discussion of the evening from family economics to science, and said, "Do you know, boys. This is a thermometer. We'll keep it in the thatch! We'll examine it in the morning. I was reading sometime back - add thirty seven to the number of times the grasshopper makes chirping sound per second. You'll see that that is exactly the temperature of the atmosphere in Fahrenheit. Did you know about this? Listen to me – I'll explain the meaning of science …."

The dilated eyes of the boys became smaller again – with a new, live curiosity! They come alive again – hope – wonderful programme for the next morning!

Everyone's eyes were filled with curiosity by that time.

Bhabaniprasad looked with satisfaction at the boy who was on course to become a scientist.

He said, "Do you remember, father? I used to examine these plants and insects in childhood. Wasn't I saying that I would be a famous doctor when I grew up?"

Bhabaniprasad's eyes closed again. Looking tangentially at Bibhuprasad, he said –

"But do you remember? When I brought you from the village for the first time after the death of your mother – did I not show several things to you standing near the Anshupa Lake – those soft and red leaves … the flowing water of the lake … the lilting songs of the fishermen of Anshupa – the small boats … the fish shining in the water … the bleating of the kids of goats in the forests … tiny, coloured wings of birds … dew on the grass below the feet … do you remember? That evening you told me – 'Father! I've written a poem. Would you like to see it?'

"Your eyes were sparkling … and I had recognized you then. Why … I had not been able to see any sign of you becoming a doctor at that time from those eyes!

Bibhuprasad fell quiet. The grasshopper fluttered in his fingers. He was not even aware when the grasshopper was taken from his hand by his brothers. Bibhuprasad felt lost for a while. Then he recovered and started arguing with his father with renewed vigour.

Even then, the problem could not be resolved – science or arts, arts or science. Bibhuprasad became restless.

THREE

There was a quiet pandemonium in the tea club of the department by two o' clock in the afternoon. An anonymous letter had arrived! The target was Prof. Jena – that baldheaded, toothy professor – professor of Bibhuprasad and others.

But Bibhuprasad and Natabar were sitting in the tea club before all these whisperings began.

It was a small room in a corner – on the first floor. One could sit near the window and see the open playground on one side, the 'avenue' of rows of deodar trees, and a portion of the college lawn on the other side. It was possible to sit there and observe people running here and there. Innumerable students! New faces – new colours. New smiles! Variety of smiles! Variety of moustaches and clothes. Oriyas, Bengalis, Telugus, Tamils, Punjabis, Hindustanis, Gujaratis, Kashmiris. A strange cosmopolitan mixture! And a small stream of water was visible on this side! By the side of the botanical garden. There was a drain on the other side of the street. A pungent smell came from the drain. A terrible smell – H2S?

Photographs were hanging all around the walls. The photographs of department heads were on two sides. However, one side of the wall – the one on the side of the college lawn – was reserved for those who were the subject-matter of discussion between the two friends that day – Bibhuprasad and Natabar.

"Who's that?" Natia asked.

"Who? That is Kekule – the one who dreamt one night that a snake came … it came and turned around to swallow its own tail! The world came to know in the morning that the shape of the benzene atom was like a ring – 'ring structure'! This is the same fellow, no?"

"Oh no! I'm not talking about those Kekules or Tekules! Where are you staring like an idiot! Look over there. Who is going? Isn't she that Murasha? There, there – she's hidden now behind the sun dial – she's coming out now – oh no! She's gone! Ah, hell! Who has located this tea club in such an awkward place! Only a portion is visible from the beautiful lawn!"

"Where? Where?" Bibhuprasad got up from the chair and ran to the window. He released a deep sigh. His weighty breath fell down without making a sound – to the ground. A little bit of carbon dioxide. Weighty – it was much heavier than air!

Tea came. Harish, the old peon, carried tea and put it beside them.

"What do you say, Sir?" Harish's voice sounded hoarse, "How about some sweets?"

"Who should celebrate? You or me?" Natabar said while sipping tea.

Harish's daughter had passed matriculation that year and enrolled in college. For some reason, the old man looked sideways at times at Natabar – a bit hungrily. Natabar was aware of that. Hence, he made fun of him at times.

"No Sir. Not me. It's you. You published a new paper – everyone was talking about you just now – Prof. Haranath had his tea and left just a while ago. What was the paper? In which journal was it published?" Harish ran his hand over the back of Natabar as he said this.

"All right, Sir. Continue with the good work. Bring glory to this college ... Haranath Babu and others were praising you a great deal just now. Are you really so intelligent?"

Harish dusted Natabar's back with his bony hand. A bit of dust had gathered on the torn collar of the shirt worn by Natabar. Harish dusted that and went away. Several teachers had gathered on the other side. Perhaps the sensational news of the day was being discussed there; but Bibhuprasad and Natabar had not been able to hear the news until then.

But their conversation was proceeding towards that. Natabar fell silent for a while after Harish left. Sipping the tea absentmindedly, he said, "I recall my uncle for some reason when I see this old man. He is one person who is etched in my memory. He used to bring books for me in my childhood when he came to the village from Calcutta ... he used to pat me on the back in this manner and said ...."

"Your uncle was in Calcutta? Have you ever been there? My grandfather worked for Calcutta Corporation after returning from the War in 1918. But he didn't bring books for us. He used to bring strange toys for us – and most of the time, he used to bring new fruit plants for his garden in the village – half of it stayed in our house and the other half went to his. The old man always ran his hand over my back and used to say, 'You'll be a judge some day'. I don't know the reason. Why was the matter of becoming a judge raised along with toys and fruit plants beat me!" Bibhuprasad picked up the thread from Natabar.

"But my uncle was the gardener of a European owner of a jute mill. I look exactly like him – I think the adage 'men resemble their uncles' is literally true. He was a good-humoured man. You know? He even flirted with the memsahib. When my uncle came to the village – you should have seen the things he carried back with him – dozens of handkerchiefs, neck ties, and perfume! Wow! Even the day before he died, he received a letter from New York which started with the word 'Darling!' I still remember it!"

"Where did he die? In Calcutta?"

"Why, no! He died in our village. He had already retired from his job by that time … there were festering all over his body. Of course, he died from insanity; but brother, that letter with the New York stamp on it! Ah! What fragrance that letter had!"

"Did he catch that disease from that memsahib?"

"Oh! To hell with that disease. I don't think he caught it from her. Uncle worked in another company after the sahib left – the sahib had found a much better job for uncle before his return – the disease was perhaps from that place. Forget it! I've never thought about that disease. I've always talked to you about the fragrance of the blue lily and the Kathachampa flower – it was that fragrance! I cannot forget that fragrance throughout my life. In the village, all of us children – girls and boys together – went out to gather flowers for the Khudurukuni Osha. The Osha was celebrated on Sundays in the month of Bhadra according to the Oriya calendar. The dawn was yet to break. Oh! Those days seem so romantic now. We swam in the ponds to gather the lily. Our place is full of water everywhere in the month of Bhadra - very strange land that Talamala is – you might have seen a picture! Saraswati sitting on a swan … a huge lotus – white lotus … everything is white there, and there is a green layer below – water! Even now I can feel that water of Bhadra – on my body!"

"But Saraswati Puja does not come in the month of Bhadra …." Bibhuprasad looked at the empty tea cup of

Natabar and smiled, "Friend! This is not ethyl alcohol – it is tea. Plain Brooke Bond tea! Of course, if it's not adulterated by the mixture of shoe leather dust."

But Natabar had no ears for Bibhuprasad's banter. He roamed in his own special mysterious world at that time –

"Thoroughly drenched – dewdrops on the heads – there were a number of girls with us – all were sisters or aunts related distantly – of the same age – it was almost morning – all of us were walking together side by side – boy and girl – girl and boy – the bodies had to touch. For we were surrounded by all kinds of witches.

"The flowers smiled from the baskets. Drops of water and dew fell from the soft petals of the blue lilies. And the Kathachampa? It's called wood of course; but it's not wood, brother, it's not wood – what fragrance!

"Suddenly, I felt something sticking in my trouser pocket. I still retain that bad habit. I had once taken a bath with the matriculation certificate in my trouser pocket.

"But that day I discovered a paper pulp in my pocket. But there was another undamaged paper – the ink had rubbed off a bit though – but one could easily read it … 'Darling!' …that letter of uncle had amalgamated with the fragrance of the blue lily and the Kathachampa flower. But I wasn't able to read anything further – the other paper had turned to pulp. I couldn't read that – what was it and who had stuck it in my pocket … on that Bhadra morning…."

Their conversation was heading towards quite a romantic consequence. The caffeine alkaloid (the chemical property of tea) in the tea was running amok in their veins.

Mr. Sethi joined them at this time.

"Hello! Bibhuprasad! Natabar! Have you heard? Your old man is dancing around. Have you seen the letter? Hasn't the old man shown you yet? Strange! The whole department is stirred up – that rosy envelope! And that letter is full of fragrance – don't you know anything?"

"What letter?" Natabar asked in a frightened voice.

Mr. Sethi was laughing. There was that innocent look on his face. But there was the smile of the limitless years on his lips – from 18 to 80! Naughty and intelligent too!

It was difficult to pin Mr. Sethi down. He slipped from inside the fingers like jelly – here one moment, gone the next.

Natabar was quite anxious. He was apprehensive that some such rosy letter had arrived for him from somewhere and found its way to the old man.

But it was Bibhuprasad who had actually started to shake with fear. For some reason, he was sure by that time that the letter was meant for him and the most dangerous thing was that the old man had laid his hands on it.

"It's all over now! My research has gone to the dogs!" Bibhuprasad could not contain himself any longer and blurted this out. "I've been telling my father! I've no plan of marrying now. On the whole, that word is not to be uttered at this critical juncture. It's all gone! I'm ruined!"

Natabar looked at Bibhuprasad, wide eyed. He was somewhat reassured. Even then his heart was thumping quite fast. Holding his breath, he asked, "So the letter is meant for you?"

With his head lowered, he answered in an embarrassed voice, "Who else? I know – I'm humiliated in this manner just for that one man!"

Something happened to him then. He got agitated suddenly and said, "I know! That one man is after my hide from childhood! Oh! Oh God! There is no respite. And he calls himself my father! The man never wanted that I should have studied science! He has been after me for ages!

I'm sure that my research is over! Who asked him – to bring up such a proposal without my permission! Father! Fah!"

Mr. Sethi laughed. There was a bit of rustic jest in his laughter.

Bibhuprasad became even more agitated. He continued in the same vein –

"You people do not know my father! He is capable of anything. Once – I was in the village and he was working at some distant place. He wanted to see me. But he was not sure that I would come to him if he called me for no reason. He asked someone else to write a letter to me, 'Come quickly if you want to see your father!' Oh, no. Do you have any idea how I felt on getting that letter? I felt as if someone was calling me from space, crying all the time ….'Ha Ram, Ha Ram' – in the voice of Maharaja Dasarath of Ayodhya! This is also perhaps a trick like that! As he could not persuade me to marry, he has perhaps tutored that girl …!"

Mr. Sethi suddenly looked somber. His face was dark. He said angrily, "Bibhuprasad! Don't blame the old man without knowing anything. I know … I've seen your father. I've talked to him. He doesn't break down at every silly thing like you. Why … he talks a great deal about you. He wants to send you overseas. He has no objection to you turning out to be a famous scientist. But he also wants that you should be a great speaker and deliver nonstop lectures … he says many such things about you. But why do you condemn him like this today? And that letter … do you have any idea about that letter? Why has it come and for whom it is meant? There's politics behind it!"

"Politics!" Natabar could finally manage to mutter. Bibhuprasad asked eagerly, "Whose letter is that? The old man's?"

"I've been saying that from the beginning! And it's

anonymous on top of that!" Mr. Sethi ordered Harish, "Hey, Harish! Serve one more cup of tea to everyone. One cup doesn't seem to work with these people."

Manmohan barged in suddenly like a rail engine entering a station yard. There was a large envelope in his hand – By Luft Post – a letter with the post mark of the German Airlines. He was followed by a number of young lecturers – eager to know about the letter from Germany.

The second session started – in the tea club.

Manmohan took his seat after ordering a cup of tea for himself.

Manmohan fired the first salvo at Natabar. That large, blue envelope with the German post mark was before him.

"Hello, Mr. Sethi! When is your new paper going to be published? Dr. Sharma was saying that you would be awarded Ph.D. in another six months!"

Dr. Sharma was Mr. Sethi's professor and research guide.

"Really!" Mr. Sethi got up. Leaving his cup behind, he joined the group where Manmohan was sitting.

Manmohan started the discussion ignoring Natabar and Bibhuprasad.

"Is it true that Dr. Sharma said this? Manmohan, did you really talk to Dr. Sharma?" Mr. Sethi asked in amazement as that was perhaps the first incident in the history of the college when Dr. Sharma might have confided such an important thing to a student of Dr. Jena.

Wearing a loose 1960 Hawaiian and a pair of slippers, a young lecturer tried to draw the attention of Manmohan and asked in an impatient voice, "Ah! Leave it! Forget about this place! This is not a college – it's a whorehouse - people would come to blows for a 'customer' – leave it! Tell me now, Brother Manmohan! Can't I get a scholarship? I would like to go to America – the 'Place of Plenty' – request your father to do something for us people!"

Staring a bit sharply at the man, Mr. Sethi turned back to look at Natabar and Bibhuprasad. The two of them winked at Mr. Sethi. Mr. Sethi lost his composure somewhat and again seemed to be hung in space.

"Do you know? In the very near future, Dr. Sharma might ...." For some reason, Manmohan seemed unsure of himself. He looked in different directions and gulped.

Suddenly, Bibhuprasad and Natabar looked at each other's eyes and they kept their ears pricked after exchanging a sharp glare.

A live pulsation started at this time in the constellation surrounding Manmohan – countless murmurings. The long neck of everyone stretched towards Manmohan.

It had all the ingredients of a real palace coup. Numerous secret parleys – fantasies – wagering – constant bickering. No one knew who belonged to which side. Hence, everyone was on guard. One or two left the place in a frightened state thinking, "How does it matter to us anyway? We're teachers – small fries. We're shrimps – if someone squeezes our heads ...!"

Mr. Sethi was not sure whether he should be happy or sad. But he broke down with some unknown apprehension.

"Manmohan's father! My God! He can get anything done," a young lecturer said as he took the blue envelope from Manmohan's hand, "But you'll see how the department will be run now. Just let Dr. Sharma come as the Professor and Head."

But Mr. Sethi could not keep quiet. He tried to protest faintly, "But Manmohan! Is this true? How could this happen? While Dr. Jena is still around ...."

Manmohan was quiet. He was examining the spots

where his 'terykhaddar' shirt was torn. He examined the faces of his audience at intervals with his foxy eyes. No one knew – whether he was unhappy or happy.

But Natabar had become very apprehensive by that time. Mr. Sethi had been shivering with some unknown fear.

Manmohan said in that deceitful, duplicitous voice, "But Dr. Jena has assured me – Ph.D. is for sure!"

"And Dr. Sharma too," a young lecturer joined in, laughing.

"In that case, it is a D.Sc.!" Mr. Sethi said in a faint and weak voice.

Suddenly, Manmohan went berserk. Looking at Mr. Sethi, he said, "But I don't bother for these cheap Ph.D. and D.Sc. degrees. My objective is not to do research. I'm only interested in the increments that these degrees will fetch for me. But I don't care about the money either. I value self-esteem. This is the greatest thing for a man. If I wish, I can buy dozens of Ph.D. and D.Sc. degrees from America and England now – even the Nobel Prize."

These were a few moments when the haughtiness of Manmohan exceeded that of even the arrogant and proud Duryodhan.

Natabar was quiet all along. He knew why Manmohan was upset. In spite of all Manmohan's entreaties, Dr. Jena had given precedence to Natabar's paper and recommended it to the journal with glowing words. He had said, "Manmohan! It would be better if you waited for a while. The Ph.D. degree should not be commercialized in this manner and one should be awarded at a time. Have patience! Let Natabar go first."

"Why Sir? Why should Natabar go first?" Manmohan's voice shook a bit at that time listening to that strange comment of Dr. Jena.

"If you and Natabar are two wrestlers and there is a tie between you, I'll judge that Natabar is the real winner," Dr. Jena said.

"Why, Sir?" Even Bibhuprasad could not digest that argument of Dr. Jena.

"The reason is simple. If your muscles have been fortified with five kilograms of mutton, a dozen chicken, one hundred eggs, two litres of milk, a basket of apples and assorted vitamin drinks, Natabar's muscles are made of a few grams of watered rice and some spinach. Tell me now, which muscles are really praiseworthy and efficient?"

It was of course a strange argument. But Dr. Jena was in the habit of putting forth such strange and humorous arguments before his students. But alas! Those were not the days of arguments or humour. Those were the days of self-esteem. And could those moments ever be forgotten – by a Manmohan?

FOUR

The laboratory closed at around eight thirty in the evening. The professor usually sat till seven thirty in his chamber. Then he got up. He came to the laboratory everyday before going home. He inspected the work done by the three students.

One had to be on guard at this time. Bibhuprasad, Natabar and Manmohan – they kept themselves busy at their work.

Nine in the morning to nine in the evening – twelve hours. This was the time when the laboratory came alive. The burner kept on burning incessantly – drums of kerosene gas! Gallons of water kept flowing. Myriad chemicals kept flowing through the drain. It was not possible to keep account of the quantum of acid and chemicals that had flown down the drain. Products of EMerck from Germany, Rockefeller of America, B.D.H. Company of England – and many other products from companies all over the globe. How they came from all around to be used up here!

Yes. No one else thought about all these. Only one person thought of everything. Bibhuprasad and the others did all their work using the thought process of this one person – just the way the use of the words like 'blue lily' and 'Kathachampa' evolved from the memory of Natabar. That thought process did not end with only some hackneyed words like 'motherland', 'country', 'nation', 'mother', etc. However, there was no end to the mockery, derision, plain laughter and criticism as these few words were pronounced time and again. Still, that man went on giving sermons and thinking aloud without bothering for anyone or preventing anyone from having his say. He was this bald man – one who held the laboratory together – Prof. Jena – or it would be better to use the language of the government – Mr. Jena, Reader in Chemistry.

Manmohan squeezed the arm of Natabar and said, "Watch out! *Kalyug's* Bhishma is coming out of his office."

Bibhuprasad nudged Natabar and said, "Careful! Ye twelve hundred mason brethren! Maharaj is on his way … Get busy! Get busy!"

Thuk, thuk, thuk … the sound of the hammer and the chisel increased. The small glass bulbs rose and fell in the distillation flask … *thuk, thuk, thuk, thuk* ….This was the laboratory – the Konark of the scientist.

A small 'conference' began every day at eight in the evening. Prof. Jena was in the middle. The students surrounded him. They started amid quite a solemn environment. It was as if the patient was lying on the operation table in the adjacent room, anaesthesia had been administered and the conference of specialists was going on in this side!

But who was really the patient that lay unconscious in the adjacent room in that anaesthetic environment? For whom was there so much activity, so many wakeful nights, such hard labour? For whose health has this chemical stream been flowing incessantly – from this laboratory?

"She is your poor mother! Your country! Your nation!

"Her life depends on the correct use of the weapons in your hands! Remember my beloved students – spare a thought for the numerous skeletons buried under this laboratory! They died – because they did not get enough food to fill their stomach. They died – because of fever and dysentery – for want of a drop of medicine. There was no space in their thin waist even to stick a pouch – not a stretch of cloth. They died – because they were unable to show their hospitality to floods and droughts every year. They died – because it was beyond them to appease the messengers of kings and zamindars."

The brightness of the electric bulbs increased as the night progressed. The students became fidgety. Prof. Jena's voice turned feeble gradually.

The three students went along with Prof. Jena till the end of the verandah to see him off. The professor took to the road.

He vanished into the dark playground.

The sound of the shoes was not audible for long.

Manmohan heaved a deep sigh and said, "Bye, bye! Pessimism personified!"

After a while, they dispersed. But they usually walked together till the college portico and to the college gate after that.

Flowers were dropping down from the two Muchukunda plants near the portico. The chirping of the birds had stopped from inside the dense leaves of the deodar trees near the college gate. The historic gate was silent without the constant chirping of the birds.

That scene and experience were awe-inspiring. Every swing of the breeze, every floating dust contained history, history and history. Why, no! Not only history! There was a lot of philosophy in the womb of this historic memory. Past, present and future mingled at this place.

It was that place where the sons got together, laughed, gossiped, and they also got into arguments – about the achievements of their fathers. Enmity sprouted from the arguments, and that led to violence, reprisals and disputes. Mahabharat took its birth. Again, the memorial of the friendship of the sons was built here – over the grave of the quarrels of the fathers.

And here they got together – before wishing good night to each other – three friends and three streams opposite each other – at this place, where the plaque of that memorial was affixed – near the main gate of the college.

"Good night!' Manmohan was the first to go. He didn't stop even for a moment to say a word appreciating the fragrance of the flowers or to stare at the wintry darkness or the moonlight of the wonderful evening. Alas …!

Natabar came along – till the gate. The chirpings of the bird had stopped from the trees. There was a stench instead – from the bird lime that had accumulated there for years.

Initially, the stench was terrible here – when the few tentative drops of the first rain of the year fell on the lime gathered through winter, spring and summer. The stench tried to keep the newcomers of the new session at bay – away from the gate.

But everyone got used to the smell in due course.

Ah!

Natabar bowed down near the deodar tree to pick up a handful of bird lime nonchalantly and sniffed at it. He said, "When I was a child …."

Bibhuprasad was aghast, "Hey! Damn you! What a nasty fellow you are! How can you smell that? You'll die!"

"Die! Ha! As if I would die just because you say so! My dear fellow! There was a cassia grove near our house in my childhood. Carcasses were thrown there. Vultures came in droves. We carried baskets of vulture stool from there and dumped that in the fields as fertilizer. My uncle from

Calcutta – who was the gardener of that sahib – talked to us one day about the fertilizer theory! Lots of vulture stool!" Natabar said as he grinded the bird lime to dust.

This Natabar was a strange fellow! As he listened to his story, Bibhuprasad recalled how Natabar looked that day. The day he had come to the college – with that hundred-rupee cap on his head.

In due course, they forgot about bird lime, fertilizer and other daily news to go back to the days of the cap.

Natabar said, "Do you know? Why have I opted for the science stream after matriculation? And again, why did I opt for Chemistry? Do you know how my father died? The disease is known as goiter. People suffered from that disease when there was deficiency of iodine in their food. A tumour developed in his throat and he died because of that. But I decided to opt for the science stream near this gate.

"Near this gate?" Bibhuprasad stood transfixed staring at Natabar's face. His fair face shone with the lights reflecting from the gate. Bibhuprasad said, gulping, "This is indeed a strange coincidence! Me too – my luck was tried here – science or arts, arts or science, through lottery!

"You too …." Natabar stopped short.

"You know my father!" Bibhuprasad turned around to look at the college building and said, "He would ask a thousand people before taking a decision. But who bothers for others at this age? We were coming that day from the village by bus. I had already filled in the form – Science, and Biology as the fourth optional. It takes one hour to reach this place by bus. My God! There was not a single passenger on that bus who was not familiar with our family history by the time we got off the bus that day.

"I was fear-stricken by the time I got off the bus and I was sure that I was going to be a lawyer. There were examples galore before me at the time – Gandhi, Nehru, Madhu Babu, Gopabandhu, Deshbandhu Chittaranjan … oh! I wished I could hide from my father for a while! I was about to revolt. I even thought of running away to Calcutta to try my luck elsewhere.

"We got down at this square to go to the college office. Father would stand beside me and I would strike out 'science' from the application form and write 'arts' in its place.

"We were walking. At this time, we saw a gentleman standing at the bus stand waiting for a town bus. I looked at the gentleman with a bit of curiosity. I found him taking some kind of powder from his pocket at intervals and applying it to his forehead after turning his hand around his head.

"I pointed him out to father, 'Father! He's the man to whom I had given the application form the other day.'

"'That man!' Father stopped in his tracks, 'The one who is applying ash to his forehead repeatedly?'

"'Yes. He's the man. He's the head clerk.' I said and reminded father, 'My fate depends on him – whether I would be Gandhi or Acharya Jagadish Chandra.'

"Father stopped. He stood rooted to the ground – as if the pendulum of a clock had stopped suddenly.

"The town bus came and went. The head clerk also boarded it and vanished from sight.

"'Father!' I reminded him, 'The gentleman has gone!' Suddenly, he turned towards me and said in a voice to imply that there had been no arguments on the issue earlier, 'I'll admit you in the science stream ….' He didn't even justify why he had changed his opinion. That's a mystery. And this gate is the witness to that scene."

"After that?" Natabar was curious.

They continued walking ahead.

"But there was no one at that time to give me that kind of advice. I took all the decisions myself," said Natabar.

"Then why did you join the science stream?"

"Because ... I had met a man near this gate the day I had come here to take the application form. A tall and huge man. The legislative assembly was in session at the time. Do you remember – the assembly used to meet in the college hall earlier?

"Sure!" Bibhuprasad answered and added, "Didn't we listen to the lectures during recesses? Hadn't the police manhandled us once when we had gone to see Godabarish Babu and Pandit Nilakantha?"

"That's right! There was a rumour at the time that steel test tubes would be used in the laboratories in place of glass test tubes – weren't the scientists of Orissa aghast when a member of the assembly demanded that unnecessary expenses should be reduced in the laboratories? At that time or just before that – the strike was going on at this place. You remember the strike, don't you?"

"Oh!" Bibhuprasad smiled and nodded in the affirmative.

"Okay! Father was in his last stage at that time. No – he had perhaps already expired by that time. He was dead – or not? Can't recall for a while. Oh yes, he was dead – I remember I had shaved my head at the time and an old man from my village broke into a loud wail in the market place when he saw me here at Cuttack. I didn't know him. But I faintly recalled that he was perhaps in that jatra party – the jatra party of our village – that had made my father famous. Have you heard of the Haladibasanta Jatra Party? It was famous all over India!"

"Famous all over India?" Bibhuprasad smirked looking at the shaven head of Natabar.

They were near the hotel. This was Bibhuprasad's hotel – 'Chhatrabandhu Healthy Food Mart'.

Natabar held Bibhuprasad by the hand and said, "I've never told you nor am I ever likely to tell you about the history of that cap. You won't be able to understand. But you should know that it was no ordinary cap! My father was a famous man of Orissa at that time. Have you heard the name of Orissa's 'Burunda'?.

"Burunda?" Bibhuprasad's face turned grave for a while. "Your father – Burunda ...?"

He took a pause.

Natabar smiled. He gulped a bit and answered in a grave voice, "No – My father's name was Ola Raut. Not Burunda. It was sad that he could not become 'Burunda'. Burunda's nearest rival – Ola Raut! My father went to far off places with the jatra party the year 'Burunda' got gold medal from Kolkata – Allahabad, Lucknow and even Banaras! Those were the days when he was in his elements. He was known as 'The Last Kharavela of Orissa' .When we were reading Kharavela's story in the village school in our childhood, the teacher always used to say, 'Oh no! Poor Ola Raut got afflicted with goiter – his throat cracked. Or else, if you want to see a princely countenance, go to Haladibasanta. If you can't see a tiger, see a cat! If you can't see Kharavela, watch Ola Raut!' Do you know who that cap belongs to? It's the cap of the Prince of Oudh! It's the cap of a Hindu king of Ayodhya. I don't know much about it. But the year I threw that cap in Mahanadi, I had gone home the same year during Dussehra. Mother started cursing me the moment she heard about it. She whined at that time, 'What did you do? You ruined your father's name!' And so forth. Forget it!"

Bibhuprasad waited for Natabar for a while. He was

aware of what he was going through. There was no way he could get rid of him before midnight and especially when he started on some ancient, historic and sensational topics like the story of his cap.

Natabar – a bottled-up, romantic personality. Sometimes, he broke down like a tornado on the mass of water of the pacific, green and crimson sea of Bibhuprasad. He churned the solemn mass of water of the sea with a roar. The water on the bed came to the surface and the water on the surface went to the bed. It turned the masts of ships abruptly. Bibhuprasad remembered – the story recounted by his grandfather about one such tornado in the Arabian Sea – the accident of a damaged war ship. A tea party was in progress on the dock. The tornado came. In a moment it ran through the ship like a sharp revolving saw splitting the ship in two parts. Shrieks were heard from the two separate pieces of the ship. The waists of a few people were still swinging – rock n' roll!

Oh! What a terrible scene it was!

As he tried to enter inside the 'Chhatrabandhu Healthy Food Mart', Bibhuprasad's head often hit that sharp bamboo sticking out from its low roof.

"Sir! Sir! Watch out!" Basudev, the owner of the hotel, cautioned him time and again.

Basudev had known Bibhuprasad for a long time. At one time, this man worked as a peon in his father's school. Now he was a big man!

"When is the old sir coming?" Basudev asked.

Bibhuprasad knew why Basudev was so interested in his father. His father came at intervals to pay off Bibhuprasad's debts. He also said, "Take care of the boy please. He's in your charge here. Look at him … how he's bent from the waist because of irregular eating habits since childhood. Make sure he has two square meals a day." Bhabaniprasad touched Basudev's lips with his fingers while pleading with him.

Hence, Bibhuprasad remembered the warnings of his father before entering the hotel every day – "Walk straight! Head up! Why are you turning into a hunchback? I had a forty inch chest when I was your age. I got appointed as a police sub-inspector in my first attempt at the age of twenty or twenty one. It was 1921! And what about you people now?"

Bibhuprasad always straightened up before entering into the hotel as if he was hypnotized. That stinking drain in front of the hotel, a mangy dog, the smell of low quality rice from within the hotel … all these acted as catalysts for that straight walk of Bibhuprasad. Hence, his head hit that bamboo without fail.

However, the various weighty personalities of the Puranic stories narrated by Natabar that day agitated him a great deal more to cause that everyday accident rather than the stench of the rice cooked inside the Healthy Food Mart.

As he sipped spoonfuls of watery dal, Bibhuprasad recalled that tall and hefty man about whom Natabar spoke often – mostly when he tried his best to glorify science.

Bibhuprasad recalled those words of Natabar. He was saying, "I had been captivated by that man and that incident. I always had a different view of myself even if I was a rustic kid. To tell you the truth, I had no idea until then as to what was I.A. or I.Sc., who was a professor, reader or lecturer, or what a pay scale meant. But there was a headmaster in our village school whose name was followed by the word B.A. (Hons.). I had fallen in love with the sound of that word since my school days. The word I.Sc. also sounded weightier than the word I.A. That was the only impression I had carried in my mind when I had come to collect the application form that day. I ran into that man all of a sudden that day.

"Fifteen minutes! I met him just for those fifteen minutes. We didn't talk. I only saw him. That was it! I've often told you that I had a strong sixth sense. And that got activated instantaneously at the time. I kept my ears pricked – just as an intelligent businessman can foresee the demand for his goods by keeping his ears pricked.

"Lots of students were moving around in groups behind this gate and that tall man too kept moving among them. I had no idea until then that it was that students' strike – the strike of 1951 protesting against the hike in college fees. I was in the muddle without being aware of it.

"By that time, it had totally escaped me that I was there to take admission in the college. I had been simply following that man. For some time, he vanished inside the assembly hall. I waited for him outside.

"A group of students outside the assembly hall suddenly started heckling someone. I realized that the tall man was their target.

"Word spread after a while that the man had torn a bundle of currency notes into shreds inside the assembly hall.

"'Inside the assembly hall? Under the very nose of the government? Over! The man is finished! He's torn legal tender. Good! Let him go to jail now!' The students started making angry noises.

"I was curious. I wondered – could it be true? The ground shook beneath his feet as he stomped around just a while ago. And this assembly hall can put him behind bars for such a flimsy reason! This is certainly no mean place – this assembly hall!

"But I was sad for some reason. Was he really going to be arrested? I don't know why I was so sympathetic towards the man. It was perhaps because of the fact that everyone who had gathered there rooted for his blood!

"A moment later, I saw that man rushing out of the assembly hall.

"'Who's he?' I asked someone.

"That boy seemed to be in a foul mood. He glared at me and said, 'Don't you know him? He's the Avatar of Kali!'

"Avatar of Kali! I looked confused. The man was saying something standing amid the enraged students; but no one seemed to be listening to him. They were only shouting, 'Clobber the rascal!'

"But I could see that all those boys only bleated like sheep around him. No one dared even to touch him.

"Suddenly, the man pushed through the students to forge ahead.

"I followed him; but I could not proceed in the crowd … I heard a noise a little bit later.

"A group of students stood near the chamber of the Principal and shouted. Apparently, the tall man had threatened the Principal, and called their revered Principal a wooden horse. This had hurt the self-esteem of the students.

"I remembered at that time that I had not come to witness the scene of the strike. I had come to take admission in the college.

"At this time, I saw the tall man rush by me.

"The students and a few lecturers had been staring transfixed. Kali's Avatar had been pushing through the crowd like a Hitler!

"I heard at this time – someone was saying – I think

it was our Dr. Jena … although he hadn't turned bald at the time … he was perhaps saying, 'Look! This boy was our student … and how he talks to the Principal now! We venerate the Principal as the most powerful person of the institution ….Oh! What has this world come to!'

"I remember that I had asked an extremely foolish question that day to Dr. Jena, 'Sir, who is this man who abused your Principal just now? What is his educational background?'

"I can still recall that glare of Prof. Jena. I had no idea at the time that this was the same Prof. Jena under whose guidance I was to work a few years later on my thesis.

"Dr. Jena's face had turned as pale as that of a man who is stripped naked and brought before an audience to deliver a lecture. He said unenthusiastically, 'I.Sc.! Once upon a time, he was a student of science ….'

"Four days later, I filled in the application form for admission to the college –

Name – Sri Natabar Raut

Father's Name – Sri Ola Raut

Stream – I.Sc.!"

Bibhuprasad had finished his dinner by that time. Basudev, the hotel owner, sat near him and counseled him as on any other day –

"Now, son! You're about to complete your studies. You're going to be a big man! Give some rest now to the old man. Find a job. Get married and set up at home. Let the old man breathe easy. He's not saying anything. But, whenever he comes here, I get the impression that that is what he wants. I believe the old man is losing out to life. The sons should now think of the father!"

Bibhuprasad felt an electric shock going through him. He went to the bank of the Mahanadi every day before he called it a day. He sat there a long time staring at the river. All kinds of thoughts crammed his head at this time.

The water of the river kept hitting the stone embankment. This was it. The river that he had been seeing since his childhood. His companion from those days. And his father might also be staring towards the bank on this side sitting in that single room beside the school hostel on the other side of the river bank.

He shivered all of a sudden. He could hear the warning of Basudev, the hotel owner, "The old man is losing out to life!"

FIVE

But that long, fruitless student life of Bibhuprasad – starting with class two in the lower primary school in 1942-43 – and facing several obstacles en route in the form of the Indian National Movement, Second World War, epidemics, death of mother, personal illness, financial trouble, etc. but still progressing somehow till 1960-61 – some days, his world went topsy-turvy amid the ineffectual research on cassia oil.

A man arrived that morning suddenly at Bibhuprasad's place. This man ordinarily came in the first week of every month from the village. Lowering the bag from his shoulder, he paid his respects to Bibhuprasad and said, "The old lady has sent these. There is *chuda* in the bag and ghee in that bottle – watch out, it may spill. There are a few pears too – those damned bats leave nothing on the trees! And now there is a bunch of monkeys. They had vanished some time back when someone had fired a few shots in the air. But they are back again ...."

Bibhuprasad asked, "How is the old lady? Is she still suffering from acidity?"

"She always complains of heartburn. Acidity is not something that is likely to go away," the man answered. He picked up the milk of magnesia bottle bought for the old woman before leaving and said, "The old sire had written that money for your examination fees will arrive shortly when the paddy is sold. But your uncle has also written from Calcutta that he needs some money ...."

But a terrible deviation was seen that day in the well-regulated life of that researcher – Bibhuprasad's.

The man arrived that morning at Bibhuprasad's place, breathless. Bibhuprasad understood everything upon seeing that man in that state.

And everything went wrong after that.

In a frightened voice, he whispered in Bibhuprasad's ears, "Sir, we're ruined!"

And then he looked at Bibhuprasad's face – for any reaction from that highly educated and dignified person.

But Bibhuprasad, who was quite adept at concealing his emotions right from his childhood, only asked that rustic, illiterate man, "Hey! Where's *chuda?* Where's ghee? Am I going to starve?"

The man was elder to Bibhuprasad; but he could never say anything harsh to him. But Bibhuprasad was aware of what went inside the mind of the man.

The man, however, tried to bring Bibhuprasad to his senses. He was a well-wisher of the family. He looked after the four to five acres of land they owned in the village. God only knew how such well-wishers sometime arrived from nowhere to help out – especially to an impoverished teacher like Bhabaniprasad serving away from home.

The man said by way of warning Bibhuprasad, "Be serious, Sir! Think of your village and the landed property sometime. The crop is bad everywhere this year – and you are talking of *chuda!* There won't be any rice to eat – nothing at all! And a bunch of touts have sneaked away with the ripe paddy standing on an acre of land – we would have harvested it in a couple of days. That bearded fellow hired about twenty goons who cleaned out the field in a flash. Please go to the village immediately – the old lady has asked you to go there and lodge a complaint in the police station. Make sure that Sec. 144 is invoked and the goons restrained. Otherwise, there won't be anything left this year."

Bibhuprasad started for the laboratory, determined not to pay any heed to the man's words. Watching Bibhuprasad walk away nonchalantly, the man called from behind and said, "The other day you were saying that one of your friends has joined as a police officer. The old lady has asked you to do something immediately. If you don't send the police to the village to go after those goons, even your homestead will be seized. Heed my warning!"

There was no answer from Bibhuprasad still. His only thought then was to somehow get inside the Healthy Food Mart to gulp some snacks and tea, and to get back to the laboratory to continue with his research on cassia oil.

The man went on muttering something hoping that Bibhuprasad would listen to him. Then he went straight to the fellow who took care of all legal matters in the village – case diary, seizures, criminal proceedings, Sec. 144 of the IPC, Sec. 145 to countermand that, decrees and sundry other eloquent words.

Bibhuprasad reached the laboratory. The taste of snacks made in toxic oil still lingered in his mouth. Hiccoughs came time and again. His dysentery-prone stomach continued to make a myriad of sounds. Pain intensified in his stomach and he felt like vomiting. But he ignored these and concentrated on his work.

The dirty cassia oil had been distilled in the mean time. A bit of pale yellow liquid. It was the result of his nonstop struggle of the past few months. But what was he going to do with that? Yes, he would examine the properties of the product. After that? He would then extract an unknown product and start examining its properties. And after that? He would produce the grandson, great grandson and great great grandson of cassia oil in this laboratory and continue his research until he discovers their properties. That was his research!

Suddenly, he felt like vomiting. He ran near the tap and tried to get a hold of himself after having a wash. The retching was obviously caused by the reaction of that poisonous oil inside his stomach.

Such retching came when the large wings of the albatross of his imagination finally felt exhausted. The eyes, which could see far, were tired of gazing at the sea below stretching till the horizon and the limitless skies above. Finally, the albatross started out in the quest for land. And because of its strange habit, it finally found an uninhabited island where it was forced to touch down.

And, at this time, Bibhuprasad pricked his ears hearing someone's footsteps outside. He shivered as if touched by the feathers of a peacock.

The sound of footsteps stopped all of a sudden – at the door of that lonely laboratory of Bibhuprasad.

"Is Manmohan Babu there?"

And a girl arrived in front of him suddenly, stupefying him in the process – Murasha!

Murasha!

Bibhuprasad seemed to have lost his tongue. There was no strength in it to form any word. There was only the taste of a seven-coloured fruit in it.

"Isn't Manmohan Babu there?"

Murasha, a student at the college, pronounced those words as if pinching the tongue of Bibhuprasad that was savouring the fruit.

Bibhuprasad said with a start, "Oh! You're looking for Manmohan Babu?"

Of course, the girl didn't laugh at the stupidity of Bibhuprasad.

Of course, she was not the kind of girl who made fun of boys nor did she make her long eyebrows dance while mouthing the gist of a college education with clenched teeth, "Stupid – nonsense – idiot – so on and so forth."

No. Murasha was not that kind of a girl. She was indeed a soft girl whose fragrance Bibhuprasad had smelt a number of times during the course of a conversation – the blue lily and the red Kathachampa! No. It was not the same blue lily and the Kathachampa flower of Natabar! Even though Bibhuprasad used those borrowed words of Natabar for this girl, the two words had by now turned out to be Bibhuprasad's very own – his very own.

Of course, Bibhuprasad knew the girl very well and he was also aware how much he could treat the girl as his very own. But he didn't know how much the girl knew of him.

The girl could wait no longer – in that lonely laboratory – waiting for an answer from a mute spectator like Bibhuprasad. As she left, she said, "Please tell Manmohan Babu that 'I' had come. Kindly take this trouble for me if you don't mind."

Bibhuprasad remained quiet. Of course, there was no need for a reply.

"Please tell him that I had come to find out about my application for the post of an air hostess. Manmohan Babu had promised me that he would get me a recommendation letter from his father – kindly remind him about it."

After that, Murasha's red Kathachampa lips attacked Bibhuprasad suddenly – like an enchanted flower. Murasha vanished in to the thin air. And Bibhuprasad's stomach started getting cramps yet again.

Bibhuprasad returned – he returned again to his pale yellow cassia oil. His stomach cramped again; but his mind now peacefully and silently pursued future research on cassia oil.

But he could not proceed any further. Bibhuprasad faced a new form of attack just as the footsteps of that girl receded from the verandah of the laboratory.

Bibhuprasad felt confounded as he was about to face that attack. The sound of shoes could be heard from the other side of the verandah. And Prof. Jena barged in like a tornado – towards Bibhuprasad.

Bibhuprasad was amazed – why should that girl come at such a lonely moment – when he had no partner to share the reprimands. Both Natabar and Manmohan were away at the time. Where were they? Why were they absent?

But Prof. Jena, the research guide of Bibhuprasad, arrived near him without giving him any further chance to mull over the matter.

Prof. Jena slumped into a chair in a lifeless manner in front of Bibhuprasad and a noose came swinging from nowhere – towards Bibhuprasad's neck.

"Who is that *woman*?" Bibhuprasad could never put up with that utterance of Dr. Jena.

Bibhuprasad remained quiet. According to a spiritual tradition, it was not permitted to give a straight answer to the research guide's question – in Dr. Jena's laboratory. Bibhuprasad was very much aware that such a course of action was suicidal. Hence, Dr. Jena could not know who that *woman* was and why had she come to the laboratory. He would also never know how a girl studying in that college, who happened to be the daughter of a poor farmer and the sister of an impoverished nurse, was concerned at the time in arranging a recommendation letter for herself. He would never know what thrill an alluring advertisement for the job of an air hostess in Air India was creating in the mind of that ambitious woman – as also among the researchers who were linked to her.

The admonitions of Dr. Jena had almost run their course in the mean time. He again warned him before leaving, "Look Bibhuprasad! Remember that one thing in life – character and sincerity ...."

But for some reason Bibhuprasad was not inclined to laugh at the grammatical error made by Dr. Jena. He was irritated and wished he could get away from this dry and pessimistic life.

But where could he go?

What other options were available to him? A job? A job meant the job of a lecturer! Cramps started again in Bibhuprasad's stomach. The *wadaas* made in toxic oil reminded him again about the warning of Prof. Sethi –

"Be careful! Eat anything. But never touch anything made of black gram. There's a couplet in Sanskrit which says that you turn into an idiot when you eat *wadaas!*"

"Does that mean one would only drink milk?" Bibhuprasad shot back only to listen to that stock sarcastic answer time and again.

"Yes, milk! But it would be wonderful if you could get donkey's milk. Very sweet and healthy."

Forgetting about the job of a lecturer, Bibhuprasad now looked in another direction – where there was a glut of the use of words like Sec. 144, touting, seizures, decrees, etc.

Yes, this was that village – wherefrom lakhs like him had fled in order to save their lives; but it was also that village wherefrom his breakfast and snacks came regularly – *chuda* and ghee – carbohydrate, protein and fat!

For some inexplicable reason, Bibhuprasad always thought about his village at hungry moments like these – from which he had distanced himself from concentrating on his studies and his research on cassia oil – from childhood till today.

Yes, this was that village – where cholera had spread and whither his father Bhawaniprasad would be running now – after getting the news from the man who would have returned disappointed after meeting him. No – why only now? He has run in that direction all his life for almost half a century – and he is running now like some hero of history – towards that cholera!

The words of that empty-handed man who had arrived in the morning –

"Be serious, Sir! Think of your village and the landed property for a while … there would be no rice this year … there would be no rice …."

As he prepared the distilled cassia oil for the second stage of his research, he had again started to sniff those foul-smelling rinds of the cassia fruit without being aware of it. Luckily, neither Natabar nor Manmohan was present there. They were not there to prevent him from doing so or to observe that natural eccentricity of his.

Suddenly, a beautiful fragrance hit Bibhuprasad's nose. No, no – this was not a few borrowed words like that blue lily or Kathachampa. This was something more scintillating – something more sensational – the fragrance of a poem!

Bibhuprasad started reciting something humming under the breath – but what was that poem? 'Small is my village'? Perhaps. Or something more real than that – some fragrance – that bunch of coconuts of the tree brought as dowry by the grandmother or the fruity smell of a few guavas of the tree that he had planted with his own hands in his childhood? Or a couple of mangoes of the mango tree that had been named after his dead sister, the berries from the bushes by the cremation ground in the village, or fries of fish from the pond located near the village temple ... whose fragrance was it? Whose poem was that?

Bibhuprasad was not aware when his eyes had turned moist in the mean time. Somehow, many other fragrances were created from all these fragrances.

For some reason, Bibhuprasad had a start on glancing at the glowing burner by his side and the cassia oil boiling in a glass jar above it. Another fragrance came to his nose from nowhere – like the fragrance of a Banarasi silk sari – the fragrance of a sari kept in a box with naphthalin balls spread all around it.

Yes, yes – this was the fragrance of that sari which had been wounded around his mother as she was being taken for cremation – it was the fragrance of that summer vacation of 1942-43. The summer in which the hybrid mango tree had borne fruit for the first time – an unknown, tiny, black bird had been moving around their house for months at the time, and that summer vacation in which he had killed (?) that golden oriole chick with a catapult!

Yes, this was that vacation and that village – where a trial was conducted after the corpse was placed on the bier – a meeting of the village chiefs was held – the husband of the dead woman prostrated himself before the village headman – and he stood there to a side after placing a mulct of five rupees - the outcaste returned to the community again after five years. The bier was lifted.

That village.

That man had asked him today to return to that village. Otherwise, he had to starve in the mornings and evenings starting today.

Bibhuprasad had been staring at the boiling oil. Footsteps could be heard outside at exactly this time. Bibhuprasad became careful.

Natabar entered the laboratory after a while. He had returned from the library. He looked sad and depressed. Perhaps he had received a letter from home.

After sitting glumly for a while, Natabar brightened all of a sudden and started out to work. Bibhuprasad could read a lot of things from his deep sighs. It could be Murasha. It could be Manmohan.

"Do you know?" Bibhuprasad teased him in order to get the truth out of him, "That girl had come today a little while ago – she was looking for Manmohan – but the old man caught me like every other day and gave the usual tongue lashing."

"Aw, to hell with your old men! I don't give a damn for them. Who is responsible for the stoppage of my research scholarship? In all likelihood, it is the handiwork of this old man. Someone was telling me today that the old man has started placating Manmohan – the reason is Manmohan has now tilted towards Dr. Sharma. The old man is now in big trouble. The other day, he was praising my muscles in order to make Manmohan look small. Now he is going to get its reward. Just wait and see. But why did they stop my research scholarship?"

Bibhuprasad was aghast. He asked amazedly, "Are they really planning to stop your scholarship? They might also do the same thing to me!"

"How do I know? You people belong to the bourgeoisie group. You ought to know that" Natabar flared up.

Bibhuprasad smiled a bit and by way of updating him with his current state of affairs, he answered, "My dear friend, what kind of bourgeoisie am I? I know you are envious of me at times because I am just a little bit better off. But all those things are over this morning. Do you know? A man had come from the village this morning. He has told me that nothing more is likely to come from the village. Those fine *chuda,* ghee, coconuts … nothing further is likely to come. Ripe paddy has been stolen from our fields."

"Good! Very good! You people deserve that. You guys think that you should clean up everything. Your father is the head master of a school. He must be making a nice pile from the school fund. This is the right time for the teachers. They are the ones who have got the villages under their wings. They would be the secretaries of the panchayats, they would be the teachers, post masters and homoeopath doctors. All loan amounts would pass through their hands – to buy fertilizers, seeds and bullocks. And there is land on top of everything else. Does your tribe plan to loot everything?"

Natabar went on with his diatribe. It was not as bad as the other days. But Bibhuprasad was extremely hurt. He answered, "My dear friend! You are talking about lower primary teachers – those who can become the secretaries of panchayats. But my father is a teacher in an M.E. school. Assistant head master. He has not been promoted as the head master even after serving for forty years. Why do you worry? Besides, you do not know my father. If you would care to come, I will introduce you to him properly."

"I know your father very well. You don't have to introduce him to me. Perhaps you do not know your own father. There is no one in this world who is more miserly than him. At least he looks like that – from his clothes." Natabar tried to lampoon Bibhuprasad.

"No, no. All of you have a wrong idea about my father …." Bibhuprasad felt slightly embarrassed and said in order to save himself, "You do not know – why do you talk nonsense all the time? My father was a disciple of Utkalmani. What you refer to as miserly and ungainly clothes is real poverty and khaddar clothes. My father has been wearing khaddar since 1921 – you do not know that history."

"I know all the people who wear khadi – don't take the pains of explaining that to me. You people have finished this country …."

"Not the kind of us, friend, not us!" Bibhuprasad's voice was slightly raised. He was even more anxious to save his skin. He said, "It's really Natabar or Manmohan – who are bleeding this country…."

"Shut up! You can't ever take my name." Natabar was not angry. But he was definitely insulted.

"In that case, you too can't take my name." Bibhuprasad was successful in defending himself. He smiled a bit and continued, "Do you know how I entered into this – this M.Sc. programme? The khaddar clothes of my father could not help me a wee bit at the time – there would be no problems for me today had I managed to enter a technical field like medicine or engineering – let a thousand professors quarrel here or let a thousand Manmohans dabble in politics here – I would not have been bothered."

After that, Bibhuprasad described those things – about which he had thought time and again on days like these since the day *chuda* and ghee stopped coming from the village. Whenever that had happened to him - from his school career till today.

This had occurred in the year in which Bibhuprasad had passed B.Sc. with honours and distinction. For the first time Bibhuprasad had been able to explain to his father in the family seminars held in the summer vacation that year that he had a natural inclination to study engineering rather than M.Sc. The first reason was that he was the grandson of an engineer. Secondly, Bhawaniprasad was aware of the fact that Bibhuprasad had shown excellence in the field in his early childhood. One of the major proofs was as follows –

A door of the kitchen used to trouble Bibhuprasad's mother a great deal when she was alive. The door hit the person opening it the moment it was opened.

That day Bhawaniprasad had assigned this problem to the child Bibhuprasad. Bibhuprasad was about four or five at the time. Bibhuprasad took just twenty four hours to fix the door in such a way that not only did the door stand still but also a bell automatically rung the moment it was opened. Bibhuprasad had not been able to explain to his father at the time as to how he had fixed the door. But the fact that a bell would ring the moment the door was opened – the event had created a sensation in that area at the time (in the language of newspapers).

However, Bhawaniprasad was not in the least interested in sending his son for technical studies in spite of all this. He was interested only in one thing – that his son should be able to make people laugh and cry at the same time by delivering nonstop lectures in English, Oriya and Sanskrit – just that one desire he had!

But, when Bibhuprasad passed B.Sc., he informed his father that it was meaningless to study M.Sc. in this country – there was no hope of getting a decent job; even a clerk's job would be difficult to find. And, in fact, many highly educated people did not find a teacher's job in a village at the time even though many promising institutions like

Hirakud and Rourkela Steel Plant had taken off in the state by then. There was a tremendous demand for engineers both in the job market as well as the marriage market. Bibhuprasad had received a long brown envelope at this time from the office of the Director of Industries. A call letter for an interview.

That day Bibhuprasad started out from home in style – as if he was going to get married. Bhawaniprasad himself helped him dress. The old maid servant of the house since the days of his mother was weeping, looking at Bibhuprasad – "Oh God! Only if his mother were alive …." She was wiping the tears.

Bibhuprasad started out in the morning on his bicycle. It was a beautiful morning. Bibhuprasad's imagination was running wild. He recalled – his mother had been prophesying one day, "Just wait and see! My son would be a famous engineer. Shaw Sahib has estimated the quantum of water in only the *Dalei Ghai;* but my son would do the same for the whole of Mahanadi."

Bibhuprasad thought about all these as he rang the bell on his bicycle. The cap on the bell shone in the sunlight. The entire face of Bibhuprasad was reflected from that shining bell. His face looked somewhat awkward and flat on the round bell. But his fair face and sharp features looked quite smart from the reflection. Bibhuprasad bared his teeth to check at intervals whether his teeth were clean or not. He was sure that they checked all these things in an interview – teeth, nails and the hair on the head ….

Just at this time, something warm and red splashed across his cheek and ran down his shirt to spread towards his feet.

He braked hard and jumped from the bicycle. His glance suddenly fell on that man driving the bullock cart –

a thin moustache, unkempt hair, striped shirt, half pant and a devil-may-care smile on the face.

Bibhuprasad burst a fuse on looking at that face. He wanted to bash the fellow up. But he controlled himself upon seeing the looks of the man. Besides, the bullock cart kept on moving. He didn't have the time to run after the man and take him to task while the spittle thrown at him by the man kept on flowing from his cheek to colour his shirt.

Bibhuprasad tried to comfort himself. Looking at the fast breeze blowing in one direction, he thought that the man had perhaps spat at him by mistake and the spittle had been carried his way by the breeze. The man was not to blame. It was all his fault. Why had he sped on the bicycle beside the bullock cart in that manner?

Bibhuprasad went to the nearby canal and washed himself. He proceeded to appear before the interview board after that.

After a while, he had to cross that line of bullock cart again. Bibhuprasad looked at the man angrily.

The man thought something – as Bibhuprasad crossed his cart, he yelled at a fellow driver for the benefit of Bibhuprasad, "Ha! If looks could kill …!"

The results of the interview were declared. The results were on the expected lines. Bibhuprasad didn't eat anything for three days and sulked.

Bhabaniprasad finally stepped out. He had that khaddar Panjabi and dhoti of 1921 on him. But there was no cap on his head. It was the office of the Director of Industries. The peon sitting at the entrance to the office stared at the fair face and the khaddar clothes for a while with the eyes of a philosopher. He thought something and saluted him. Bhawaniprasad's feet started trembling then.

He thought of something all of a sudden and came

back in stead of proceeding any further. Bibhuprasad and Aniruddha had been waiting for him outside. He called the boys to him and explained –

"Listen boys! Do you know Shauri Babu, the judge? He had applied for a job in his childhood, and failing to get it, he rolled on the floor with tears running from his eyes. His father worked as a mukhtiar. He called his son to him and said, 'Hey! You good-for nothing fellow! Why are you bawling like a woman? Come and work as a mukhtiar if you are not getting anything else. Be a lawyer! Learn the trick of talking nonstop. This world belongs to the man who can talk or count money. Shauri Babu studied law at an advanced age. And look at him now! He is Justice Shauri Babu now!'"

But Bibhuprasad didn't proceed to study law. He continued to strive to study medicine. He had also applied to the medical college for admission.

The call letter for the interview came and he started out for Cuttack. He was careful about the clothes he wore and did not forget to carry a spare set of clothes with him.

He was selected to study medicine.

Bibhuprasad's family had been filled with joy that day. There were dreams galore.

Oh! Those were the days! Bhawaniprasad did not sleep throughout the night and he didn't allow anyone else to sleep either. He kept the nine year old Aniruddha awakes by pinching him time and again throughout the night – just so he would listen to him. The major worry at the time was to arrange money month after month for Bibhuprasad's studies. At times, Bhawaniprasad expressed the displeasure of a concerned father and blamed Bibhuprasad –

"Son! You are not going to achieve anything the way you are going. You do not realize that a penny saved is a penny earned. You must learn to prune your expenses. Otherwise, you cannot do anything in your life. If you spend everything you earn …."

Bibhuprasad put forth many counter arguments – showing his shrunken tummy and torn shirt before everyone.

But Bhawaniprasad argued, "There have been many who continued with their studies by eating roots of trees and drinking water from the river. You are much better off in comparison. You don't have to worry about food at least. I've taken care of the five acres of land for that reason alone. Keep an eye on the land – I keep exhorting you all the time …."

Some dispute was going on relating to the land that year in the summer vacation. Bhawaniprasad was away from the village. Bibhuprasad was at Cuttack. Five quintals of rice were stolen one night from the store. The paddy had been harvested and buried under the earth – in order to save it from thieves. Everything was lifted during the course of a night – like the seeds being stolen from the fields of someone who had planted seeds at the time of harvest.

Five quintals of paddy – that meant four hundred rupees at the rate of eighty rupees per quintal. Bibhuprasad's study of medicine had to be stopped once this amount slipped out of hands.

Bibhuprasad still remembered his father running to court in connection with that suit relating to the theft of paddy. He had lectured a meeting of clients sitting under the banyan tree near the court and explained the benefits of science once again to his father that day.

Bibhuprasad could still recall what he had told his father that day –

"Father! I have one lifelong ambition in fact – and that

is to scale the peak in science. I'll do research, father! I'll do research and scale the peak in research to win the Nobel Prize! I'll invent medicines! Do you remember, father? My mother died; but we were not in a position to give her proper medicines. It was not simply our poverty, father! It was our ignorance. We had not even heard of penicillin that day – which is known to every kid today ...."

His father had finally smiled a bit and permitted Bibhuprasad to study M.Sc.

Bibhuprasad remembered his father and the other clients discussing something behind him as he left the premises of the court that day.

Bibhuprasad's father was introducing him to a few rustic litigants that day. He said, "Do you know the reality about this brat, uncle?

"This fellow is a poet – a poet! He writes verses. Very good verses. Would you care to listen to one of his lines? This relates to babies. This boy had written it in his childhood!

"'A new one has taken birth ....'

"Isn't it fantastic? What thought process! On the strength of this, the boy has started out today to create medicines!"

SIX

But –

The next morning –

The next morning was different.

It was that kind of morning when students like Bibhuprasad were getting out of bed, rubbing their eyes. It was yellow all around them: not the golden colour of the sun, nor the green colour of the leaves – the yellow covering the mind? Jaundice? Who knew what that yellowness was?

But thank God, it cleared off after a while. The yellow colour vanished. It was perhaps vitamin deficiency, weakness of the nerves, excessive bile!

Then they got up. No – they had to take vitamins now. More vitamins. Plenty of vitamins. Nutritious food. Some germinated gram, one ripe banana, a spoonful of scraped coconut, at least half of a half-boiled egg and at least half a glass of milk – beside the usual food.

They broke into a sprint.

"Do you have grams? Grams?" They lined up outside the grocery shop.

"Yes – what do you need? Whole ones or dal?" A thick neck boomed. Like the narrow side of a mridangam.

"Come on, what do we need dal for? We need the whole ones! Whole ones – that would sprout properly. Real sprouts. White and fresh sprouts – Vitamins A,B,C,D,E …." They stretched their necks towards the balance which had tilted towards the right.

"Hey! Are you trying to teach the alphabets to me? You think I don't know the alphabets? Only you guys going to the college have studied everything? How much do you need? Why are you trying to put on airs?" The man answered in a voice that had perhaps been designed to banish all sense of aesthetics.

"All right, give me one kilogram. What can we tell you! Times are changing …." They held the bag open. Black grams blinked at their white, greedy eyes from inside the balance held by the grocer. They had been trying to jump into the bag like a baby extended its hands to jump on to the lap of the mother. What beautiful stuff these were – each grain of gram. Much more beautiful than the image of Baby Krishna – more exciting – even rarer was that smile – that face, that colour. Grams!

"Hey! Why don't you make haste? What's the delay? We've got work to do. We'll be late for the college."

"Aw, to hell with your college! The grams are falling off from the bag. Wait a moment. Just wait. Do you have any idea how much each grain of gram costs? Why are you shouting your head off early in the morning for no reason?"

"So, you are not in a mood to sell any grams? Why don't you say so? How much time would a working man waste for a seer of grams?" The openings of the disappointed bags closed. The grams burst into an even louder laughter against their wishes inside the balance of the grocer. Oh! How terrible was that laughter!

"So, you don't want to buy any grams! Why don't you say so? We're traders sitting here. We're here to release our goods; that is our deliverance. Let's see your money. Ha! There's no sign of any money; but you're in a hurry to take your stuff."

The grocer banged the balance on the floor. He

concentrated on other customers. A few grains of gram rolled off on the floor. The customer felt as if someone smeared a handful of mud on his face. He stepped back. And the words hit him from behind –

"Don't I know this guy? Must be getting around two hundred and fifty rupees a month. And the cost of a bag of grams is a hundred and fifty rupees. Do such people ever eat anything? They only sniff at things. Look at him! He's getting delayed for the college!"

They left the place – with their tails tucked behind them. They made the calculations quietly. If it was a hundred and fifty rupees for eighty kilograms, how much did one kilogram cost?

"Oh, my God …." They walked even faster. Farther and farther away – from grams, from bananas, from milk, from eggs … farther away from vitamins. And Bibhuprasad got up from the bed yet again on one such morning.

He had slept late last night. He had borrowed a few History books from the library some days back. The books had gathered on the table. That caught his attention. He picked one up and read it. And he continued to read. He became conscious of the time at two in the morning.

Oh no! It was his job to get up in the morning and collect cassia fruits. He had to go towards a village in order to collect the fruits. He had to get up early; but here he was, reading History books late into the night.

And it was a book of British History at that!

Why?

He sat up all of a sudden. He was in an agitated state having slept very little in the night; but for some reason – he sat up like an avowed brahmachari deeply aroused sexually upon seeing the reflection of the backside of a beautiful, young woman on the trunk of a dried up tree in a forest.

There was a row of books on British History, Indian History and political science in front of him.

"I'll surely … surely …." Bibhuprasad leaned on the row of books again. He explored the row of books as if it were the image of a half-naked woman.

"I too can do it … why not …." He mumbled repeatedly.

Suddenly, his self-confidence increased manifold. The reason was that the mantra that he had made it a habit to recite from childhood before undertaking every important work also came now to help him – just at that time.

"Whatever Man has done man may do."

And he went on reading. He went on reading history pushing the chemistry books aside. British History.

It was four in the morning.

He was still awake. He continued reading and counting with his fingers … January, February, March … filling up of forms … April, May, June and August. Seven months! That was enough time. Even a small germ could take the shape of a complete human being if it could get the right environment. And why can't an intelligent man succeed in any competitive examination if he got so much of time?

He was going at double the speed at four thirty in the morning.

But, by five in the morning, the 'competitive' fever had receded to a great extent.

He had perhaps dozed off at around five thirty in the morning and seen that yellow dream in that state. He was wiping off that yellowness from his eyes that morning.

But Bibhuprasad knew very well by that time that it was not a dream – it was a stark reality, a truth! But it was not true relating to the times of Bibhuprasad! It was the truth of that age – the age in which Truth shrieked and summoned all and sundry as a contemplative young man on the sands of the Kathjodi River, "The Satyagrahis of India – unite!"

"White rulers! Quit India!"

"Bande mataram!"

"Inquilab zindabad!"

"That was 1921 ...." The firm, steely voice of Bhawaniprasad echoed repeatedly in the ears of Bibhuprasad.

"This relates to the time when Mahatmaji had come to Cuttack – a meeting was held on the sands of the Kathjodi River. Utkalmani was addressing the crowd – tears were streaming down from his eyes and his face glowed! The students had been forcibly held back in the hostel premises – strict orders of the Gora Principal and strong supervision of the black superintendent – this Mangaraj jumped through the window of the lavatory to arrive at the meeting – this Rajkrishna, who had built his muscles through regular exercise, was roaring 'we want war, we want war'- and – who was not present there? Even Bichhanda, who couldn't walk properly, came down the stairs holding on to the wall. Those terrible, exciting days ... they had called me for the post of a police sub-inspector."

"Why didn't you join, father! Oh! How can an educated man make such mistakes? You would be retiring today as an I.G. or a D.I.G.!' Bibhuprasad almost broke into tears at the time.

Minaketan, the younger brother, sat quietly, sulking. He was pouring all his complaints silently.

That was also a day at that time – when the deeds of the forefathers were judged by their dumb children. Minaketan had passed matriculation that year. Bibhuprasad was about to pass B.Sc. (Hons.).

Summer vacation has come again. Days of family meetings. Arguments started that led to quarrels and finally to pitiable decisions. The decision was taken – the wise gave up half his possessions when disaster stared in the face. Bibhuprasad studied M.Sc. and Minaketan joined a company. A lot of hope and assurances were given to him – "You will see! You will one day surpass Bibhuprasad! This is the age of science! The age of machines! Anything you touch turns into money. Enter the field, son! Enter the field of machines – if you want money, if you want to live. And there is no dearth of respect either. One can also go overseas if he does well. Let this fellow study M.Sc. and do whatever he wants to do."

This was the same Bhawaniprasad who argued with Bibhuprasad four years ago – as the eternal enemy of science! He made an about turn suddenly – by compulsion.

Minaketan agreed to the proposal like a good boy. The orders of father had to be carried out. Especially the duty-bound son of a father from the middle class – Minaketan.

The echoes of these feelings that arose in the paternal heart of Bhawaniprasad troubled Bibhuprasad on those yellow mornings.

Bibhuprasad complained again –

"All our misfortunes are because of your thoughtlessness – you are extremely cruel ancestors! A family of zamindars turned into beggars on the street because of your negligence. And you lost such a huge opportunity knowingly just because of your whims! The post of a sub-inspector those days!"

"We would be moving around in a motor car today – no, brother?" The imagination of Aniruddha hurt Bhawaniprasad at the time like a slap on the cheeks.

There is a saying – 'The son led a happy life because

of the good deeds of the parents'. The harsh comment of Bibhuprasad slashed Bhawaniprasad's skin all over; but he glowed again after brushing off the dust of yesteryears from his face. No regrets showed on that face.

Bibhuprasad remembered that face. That glow was not just the self confidence of a stupid person. It was not the ineffectual self-glory of a person who had lost all his ill-begotten wealth. It was the kind of glow in which the soul longed to bathe.

Swallowing all the complaints of the children in one gulp, Bhawaniprasad laughed that day and said –

"Forget it! Let bygones be bygones! But have you ever bothered to see what your parents have left behind for you when you children sit in the judgment of us parents? A job is like the shadow of a palm tree; but people were hoping for a more permanent shadow those days than this shadow of the palm tree. Look towards the village now. You'll see what your father has left behind for you there!"

Bibhuprasad smiled; but he did not dare make any further harsh comment.

Minaketan had been quiet until then. He opened his mouth suddenly. His sullen face gave way to expression. Everyone turned mute for a moment – at his roar.

"What do you think of us, father? Do you think we would go back to those dark ages again? Working as peons, clerks or teachers like you – from village to the city and from city to the village – holding on to an income of a paltry six rupees for dear life – running to the village on Saturdays on the ramshackle bicycle – strewing a bit of something like a squirrel, throwing something into the mouth, back again on Monday morning to hold on to the job? A bundle of rice, a packet of *chuda,* a handful of pulses and a few cakes of black gram on the shoulder. Do you still think that this is the best thing that can happen to your children? And you seem to be proud of it. What that land is worth after all? Just about three to four acres! And it is not as if you have acquired it from your own earnings. Village, village, village … what the hell is there in that village? All the time you talk about the village – and you got the cheek to tell us that you spurned the job in the police force because of the village – for the land! Why? All those who wore khaddar and Gandhi caps along with you are now stinking rich … their children can study B.A., M.A., medicine and engineering. Why should we go looking for a job in a company? Why should anyone tell us that there are paddy fields, mango groves and other such rubbish for us in the village – and we got to live on that …?"

That smile had still not left Bhawaniprasad's face; but something was trying to rise within him – it came up to the neck and could not proceed any further.

He could not explain matters to his apathetic children. How could he make them understand? The history of half a century separated the thinking of those days and today. Those days and events vanished in the stream of history like a wavelet. History could not record those wavelets.

They could not at all understand the significance of those words when Bhawaniprasad narrated them before his children. Words like khaddar, charkha, constructive work, harvesting of salt … words like these had remained unintelligible for all time to come just like the sentimental days of those yesteryears.

Bhawaniprasad heaved a deep sigh.

Of course, that deep sigh was not meant to harm anyone. It only shook the atmosphere of that closed room for a while.

He said for the benefit of the angry Minaketan –

"You would realize it some day. The four acres of land that I have been able to save from the enemies would some day come to your aid, and then you would say –'father had saved this for us, and we and our children are enjoying its fruits.'"

"But father! Do you still think that that kind of day will ever come? Would we be so poor that …?" Bibhuprasad shot back.

"Wait, son. Just wait. You would be again hearing that slogan in a few days – 'Back to the field'."

"But we can never return there."

"You have to return. Hunger would force you. The growing family would force you to return."

"We'll find jobs that pay well. We won't end up as a teacher like you to hock our heads for thirty rupees a month."

"A job means exactly that – hocking your head; but neither have I hocked my head nor am I going to do so. Had I done so, I would be an I.G. or a D.I.G. today as you mentioned."

"That would not have been so bad. An I.G. earns a hundred times as much salary as a teacher. You could have bought thousands of acres of land."

"That I had no such desire goes to show that I had no inclination to hock my head. And had I hocked my head …." Bhawaniprasad's voice suddenly turned grave and he continued in an extremely rough voice, "Had I hocked my head, how could I have called myself the father of such educated, wonderful children as you? Would I have permitted a single educational institution to thrive in Orissa to educate you people?"

"What do you mean?" The children were scared looking at that terrible face although the words had no impact on them. Bhawaniprasad's face blazed – not like a jewel – but like an iron rod burning in fire.

"What I mean is that I would have set fire to every school and would have been known as the second Kalapahada of Orissa – that was the stipulation set forth by the British government for the job of the sub-inspector."

The children of Bhawaniprasad were totally unfamiliar with such fiery countenance of their father. They sat quietly – like a few dumb children.

Sparks started flying now from the burning eyes of Bhawaniprasad.

"We are not Kalapahada! We are not Kalapahada! Destroying images is not our family business, son! Creating images – building temples is our tradition. We've been teachers for seven generations – we would remain as teachers."

Bhawaniprasad was swollen with pride. A whiff of breeze moved inside his rib cage. Then he took control of himself and appeared in the natural shape of a teacher of literature. He seemed to be reciting the poems of those poets at the time –

"Oh, you herd of beggars! Turn into human beings! Turn into human beings! Turn into human beings rather than monkeys! Learn to walk on two feet. Learn to stand with a straight back. Go – see – how monkeys turn into human beings in this world. Aren't all those men standing before you? Ask Madhu Barrister. Ask that cry-baby Gopabandhu. Go and ask Nilakantha and Godavarish. Hold their ears and ask them ….

"Folks! You took so much in your stride – you survived eating banana skin and working as cooks – with palm leaf umbrellas on your heads, you bloody Oriyas carved out a niche for yourselves at a place like Calcutta University.

But why didn't you earn enough money for yourselves by serving as magistrates or turning into the henchmen of the government by acting as spies for the police? Why didn't you count as someone in this world?

"Someone lost his eyesight by reading in the light of a lamp even as he was busy cooking and some son of a cowherd stood first in the class competing with Subhas Bose, the son of a father like Janaki Bose. Some kid survived on inedible stuff because there was not enough rice to eat and quenched his thirst by drinking water from the canal. Still, he continued with his studies and turned into someone to reckon with. Do you know him, you herd of beggars?

"Those people turned out to be the best in this age – Pati, Parija, Sarangi. And you hapless fellows are sitting here on your butts cursing your luck. You are blaming others and shedding tears.

"Why? You are not orphans like them. Only your mother has died. No – how could she be dead? She has left behind a couple of gold bangles and a gold necklace for you – to sell them off at the time of need. Your father is not destitute. He might not be a police I.G. or a district collector; but he is not destitute. He too gets something every month by way of a salary. He has saved the ancestral property of five acres of land for you fighting with his enemies since he was nineteen years old. And that enemy is not to be underestimated! It's the government itself – what was known as the zamindar and court cases at that time. And that zamindar was no pushover either! He was a lawyer and zamindar like Praharaj himself who carried magic in his brief case – it was said that he sewed up the mouth of the opposing counsel and pulled wool over the eyes of the judge.

"And this is that father of yours! He is sitting here

before you. He has never bowed his head before injustice. He has never given in to theft, larceny, bribes and falsehood.

"My son! What are you afraid of? There is a saying – 'a son never loses out in life as long as the father is alive'. Go – fly. Move around different countries. Lecture to people. Nonstop lectures. Turn into a Gandhi, a Vivekanand, a Gopabandhu or a Godavarish. Walk with a swollen chest on the path of truth, religion and independence … save this country from the darkness of utter poverty and illiteracy. Provide food to people and bring light to their eyes … these are the duties of a good son!"

Bibhuprasad got up from the bed wiping off the yellowness of the eyes. He collected the books on history and political science lying open on the bed from the previous night and put them back on the racks. Then he heaved a deep sigh – a sigh of relief.

Oh! There is no further need to count months.

I.A.S., I.P.S., O.A.S. … all these vanished from the eyes of Bibhuprasad like a few bad dreams of the sleepless night of a researcher. The desire to be a district magistrate or a superintendent of police in order to frighten grocers selling grams gradually receded from his eyes.

The sunshine of the morning, the chill air, the chirping of the birds, the lowing of the neighbour's calf, the sound of the horn of the landlord's truck … all these again sounded melodious to his ears.

Bibhuprasad started out on the village road. A few cassia fruits were needed for his research.

SEVEN

That day Natabar arrived after doing something inexplicable.

Bibhuprasad was collecting the oil extracted from the cassia seeds in a clinical flask in the laboratory. A bit of dirty reddish oil. It gave out a terrible smell. It was not only the oil. The entire laboratory stank that day of something terrible. There was the stink of pyridine everywhere. Flies buzzed everywhere.

Sitting in a corner, Manmohan was slyly going over a book to learn the German language. He went to his table at intervals. He was working on some materials akin to sugar. Sugar and related chemicals had been strewn on his table.

"Do you know, boys? I'm going to be – another Perkin in this world," he was laughing intermittently and saying that.

[A scientist called Perkin had suddenly invented some kind of colour as he did his research on Quinine. The name of the colour was 'mauve'. The history of chemistry records how this researcher on Quinine finally turned into a billionaire businessman in paints. Like the German scientist Bayer, this English scientist cornered the paint market of the world in such a way that farmers of underdeveloped countries like India who earned a few sterlings or dollars by engaging in profitable farming of indigo or red dye (kumkum) rather than rice or wheat were deprived of it. The western scientists had rendered this help to India in the last century.]

"Very good!" Bibhuprasad answered with a smile, "Perkin and Bayer had removed bangles from the wrists of the wives of our farmers. And what about you? You want to invent sugar. What would you extract it from – coal or wood? How much would a seer cost?"

Manmohan was again returning to the book of German language lying open on his table. He said, "We do not have the time to think of those things. Who cares? A scientist is not bothered about such trivia. Our job is to invent things. A Ph.D. is the first thing. A D.Sc. after that and finally, the Nobel Prize. My work is over then."

"So, you're after the Nobel Prize now! Nobel Prize indeed!"

However, in stead of allowing Bibhuprasad to savour the salty taste of his comment, Manmohan shot back, "You idiot! The Nobel Prize is won by people like you and me. The man winning the Prize is not made any differently. Laboratory facilities, an intelligent guide and a research scholar – these are the only things needed for the purpose. But neither do we have such laboratories nor such enlightened guides. Look at the prospectus of Berlin University. There are dozens of Nobel laureates in every department there. That's it – one has to find the right guide; I'm there as the research scholar. The only thing that remains is reaching that place and taking advantage of the well-equipped laboratories there. And I'm ready for that."

"Ready?" Bibhuprasad was startled. He had no knowledge that Manmohan had already prepared himself to leave for Germany. He was as amazed as sorry to hear that. What would the professor think when he learns this? The three of them – Natabar, he himself and Manmohan – had they not given the word to the old man just the other day that they would neither marry nor engage in any other work until they completed their Ph.D.? Had Manmohan forgotten that promise! So, he was going to ditch the professor!

(Of course, Manmohan's father was an extremely rich and powerful government servant. Not just for seven generations – his family decided Orissa's fate since ancient times. It is said that Manmohan's great, great grandfather was in charge of distributing relief at the time of the Na'anka Famine and the funds at the disposal of Commissioner Ravenshaw Sahib were handled by him. Manmohan's family was stinking rich since those days.)

"Listen! I know very well that a genius is not needed in this age of the specialist to come to grips with science. And I would never agree that every Nobel Prize winner is a genius. Today's science does not need intelligence. All that one needs to do is hard labour. Anyone who can engage in hard labour can win the Nobel Prize," Manmohan said while leafing through his book on German language.

"So, you're trying to say that we're wasting our time here in the laboratory? Why, our people don't get the Nobel Prize as frequently as people in other countries!" Bibhuprasad answered while preparing the cassia oil for distillation. For some reason, he was gradually getting to be envious of Manmohan. He could recall a secret divulged by Manmohan the other day as they were having a chat. Manmohan's father had shown some great favour recently to two companies with regard to their income tax obligations. Perhaps those companies were helping Manmohan realize his dream of the Nobel Prize at the time.

Manmohan had not forgotten to answer Bibhuprasad's question. He was espousing his everyday theory. He said, "You idiot! I told you once that science has got nothing to do with intelligence – it's all hard labour! Ninety per cent perspiration. And if only hard labour matters, capital will come automatically. What it means is regulation of labour is easy when capital is available in plenty. And production will be more when there is provision to regulate labour. Hence, in this age of the specialist, the Nobel Prize is also controlled by capitalism; i.e. the number of Nobel Prizes is more in that place where there is more money. This is my statistics! See for yourself – how many Nobel Prizes are won by Americans every year and how many are won by other countries!"

That a sarcastic comment could be made in the process of relating the possibility of getting the Nobel Prize to the principles of economics was beyond the comprehension of Bibhuprasad. He felt that Manmohan had started a strong philosophical criticism of contemporary science and scientists without being aware of it. And Manmohan's statement seemed to carry a lot of truth in it.

Those were the days when the children of rich men considered themselves to be fortunate if they could somehow slip out to other countries to get a preliminary degree after passing in third division from an Indian university. They knew that it would not take them long after that to beat the boy standing first in the class. It may also happen that the boy securing the last rank in the class may reach the same spot by walking where the boy securing the first rank finds himself after running for five years. The economic theory of capitalism behind a foreign university and a foreign degree worked wonders at the time.

Bibhuprasad was immersed in his work. But Manmohan had not stopped his monologue. He continued, "All the money is mine! I'm not taking a dime from the Government of India. I've got plenty of money and plenty of time. This is the game of eating cakes. The taller you are, the higher your mouth gets. And the larger your mouth, the greater the size of the cake you can grab. Hence, you're destined to win. There is no point in losing your sleep over it!"

Manmohan and Bibhuprasad heard some noise at this time from the college playground and ran outside.

Luckily, Prof. Jena was on leave that day and there were not many students near the playground.

The incident occurred at that time.

Bibhuprasad and Manmohan ran there and saw – a boy was running like a mad bull in the middle of the playground and a few people were chasing him.

It was quite a scene!

One could not stand still watching that amusing scene.

"He had perhaps entered someone's house," Manmohan and Bibhuprasad burst into laughter at the same time.

The boy running to save his life was running in circles. The men chasing him were slowing down as if they had lost their way. There was a barrage of cursing and scolding going on in foul language.

A few heads had started popping out of the staff quarters and ladies hostels around the playground.

"Look! Look! How that fellow is running in circles like the matador in the movie Quo Vadis!"

Manmohan and Bibhuprasad were laughing!

Suddenly, the boy made another swift turn for the last time like a kite diving down in the sky and vanished on the road leading to the malgodown.

The people dispersed after a while. The playground again became empty and quiet. The heads popping out of the staff quarters and ladies hostel disappeared. People forgot the stray incident in a moment. Such incidents were a common, regular affair those days near the playground. There were robberies and other kinds of petty crimes – people ran after the offenders for a while and then they kept quiet.

The incident was amusing for Bibhuprasad and Manmohan; but it was equally significant for them!

Natabar arrived after a couple of hours. There was no mark of any wound on his body. But there was a swelling on his forehead.

Bibhuprasad had finished all the preparations to distil the raw cassia oil. Natabar barged into the laboratory just as Bibhuprasad was getting ready to start work.

Manmohan and Bibhuprasad were ready to convulse with laughter by way of welcoming Natabar. Natabar slumped into a chair.

Natabar seemed unconcerned by the mirth displayed by Manmohan and Bibhuprasad. He seemed to explode rather than defend himself with his fist raised. He was mumbling something unintelligible from inside his parched throat. Suddenly, he fell down on the floor.

There was no scope for any further amusement there. It was the final outcome of a really hungry research scholar.

Bibhuprasad was aware that Natabar had not received his scholarship money for the last six months. That money could not be sanctioned in spite of several recommendations of Dr. Jena. There were some other hurdles too for him to receive the money. A rumour was making the round in the tea club at the time that the Department of Education had decided to do away with the system of research scholarship from that year as it became known that the standards of scientific research had continuously gone down over the years and the scholarship money was being misused by the scholars as well as the professors.

Bibhuprasad and Manmohan had been trying to bring Natabar back to his senses by throwing water on his yellow, bloodless face and forcing him to smell ammonia at intervals.

"We should give him a lot of water mixed with sugar! The glucose percentage in his blood has become terribly low," said Manmohan.

"Why sugar? We've got glucose with us!"

"You wait here. Let me get a cup of tea." Bibhuprasad had a worried look on his face.

"Ah! What is the use of tea? Brandy is needed – otherwise, some whisky or rum would do. This is the way to bring my father back to sense when he faints!" Manmohan laughed suddenly.

"Does your father faint often?"

"Of course, it's not hysteria …." Manmohan tried to explain about his father's fainting fits to Bibhuprasad.

As he wiped the wet face and hair of Natabar with a dry towel, Bibhuprasad was startled to see that gaunt face and the sunken eyes. Perhaps he thought at the time –

A boy worked here with him who doesn't have a father … the father died of goiter … just because he didn't get a bit of iodized salt with his food … this is Ola Raut's son … his father was the last Kharavela of Orissa.

Bibhuprasad could not look at those dilated eyes. He looked at that dirty, reddish cassia oil jar standing on his table.

"What is the need for this? Of this useless cassia oil? When no food has gone into the stomach for the last six days and the researcher has slumped here on the floor of the laboratory!"

The laboratory had become unbearable with the stench of pyridine and the buzzing of the flies. Bibhuprasad felt breathless.

Natabar's misfortune had come in this manner –

Natabar's mess had closed for the last five or six days. One of the members of the mess who had just started out as a lawyer did something because of which the five year old mess had closed. The members of the mess had a tacit understanding that they were free to do anything outside the mess; but no one was allowed to indulge in any sinful activities like drinking, whoring, wielding swords or any such act that was likely to disturb peace. There were a few poor students, a couple of clerks, one pharmacist and some such people in the mess.

Two rickshaws stopped in front of the mess one day in the middle of the night. When the other members got up in the morning, they discovered three kids sitting in a row under the verandah and passing stool. A discussion was in progress among them –

"Whose house is this, Munia? Ours?"

An old man was sitting on the verandah shouting at them, "Hey kids! Finish quickly! Stop talking and come back!"

An old woman was swabbing the earthen floor.

The members of the mess were watching transfixed.

The kids looked at their new world with bewildered eyes. Watching so many people in one place and all of them coming out of their new house – any kid would have been puzzled.

"Don't get frightened, kids – these people live with us! You would come to know each of them gradually. Okay, finish your job … don't be frightened …!"

Grandpa had started explaining things from the top of the verandah.

At this time, the great lawyer came outside, rubbing his eyes. The lawyer started explaining before the mess members had a chance to put a stern expression on their faces, "Listen to me, my brothers – don't get angry – a man moves from a pillar to post when there is trouble – who has got any control on natural calamities? We were living here in this mess like brothers. I hope you will take that into consideration. You are my brothers. Most of you are of the same age as my younger brother. You must have heard of the terrible cyclone that took place a couple of days back – it was reported in the newspapers … there are three kids and the wife is in the carrying stage on top of that … this is what a natural calamity is all about! God tests the strength of the mind and the character at such times! I brought the kids here from the village hoping that you would stand beside me in my misfortune … the village has been razed to the ground … now you are the only hope for the kids …."

The mess was closed by that evening. There was no food. The cook was not to be seen from the afternoon. The other members of the mess slipped out one by one from the next morning. Only Natabar was left. He could not arrange an alternative place that quickly. Apart from that, he was looking for a chance to have a confrontation with the lawyer. He had caught on to the games being played by the lawyer. There was no hint of any cyclone from what he could gather from the conversation of the family members of the lawyer.

Natabar had nothing to eat as the mess closed. He had already paid the advance to the mess for the month. But when he returned to the mess in the night, he heard that the mess was closed and everyone had made his own arrangement.

Natabar had clung on to the mess angrily as if someone had violated his constitutional rights. He stayed in the mess for six days eating only wadaas and samosas.

He came to the laboratory during the daytime and sat in his room in the mess from eight in the evening till one in the morning with the lights on. Two nights passed in this manner. No one said anything to him. Natabar couldn't even prevent the children of the lawyer from having a free run of the house.

Natabar did something on the third night. He carried a bit of rectified spirit with him when he returned from the college in the evening. A broken flute had been lying near his suitcase on the floor – he had bought it in his first year in college. He sprinkled the rectified spirit on the verandah – so that an alcoholic atmosphere would be created there. Then he played the flute till late in the night. Initially, he found that the lawyer's mother was getting slightly irritated by it. Perhaps the lawyer was the only son of the old woman. The scriptures said that the mother of a single son ought not to listen to the music of the flute at night; but all mothers were not Yashoda or all sons were not Krishna. The old woman gradually fell quiet. Next, the three kids started peeping through the window – Natabar watched everything.

Natabar thought the music of the flute provided them with entertainment without any cost rather than irritating them. He got angry and started blowing on the flute tunelessly. He was so irritated with his own music by one in the morning that he was not aware when the flute had slipped out of his hand and he had passed out.

Natabar was determined to move the family of the lawyer from the mess on the fourth day. Several weird ideas were playing in his head by that time having almost starved for three days and because of excessive mental excitement.

He had decided by that time that it was his life's mission to defeat that rogue lawyer. Rama and Krishna took birth in this world to destroy the wicked and save the saints. Similarly, the boy Natabar, who had taken birth in an oppressed, unknown family of farmers in a mofussil village, assumed that it was his life's calling to finish the dynasties of all thieves and touts of this country, and to restore the hijacked mess to the rightful homeless, hungry owners as also return every dime paid by them towards mess advance with compound interest.

"If needed, I'll drink alcohol and dance naked before his wife ... I'll see how he would continue to stay at this place after that." Natabar took the solemn oath that evening and he actually drank quite a bit of alcohol that night – the alcohol stolen from the laboratory.

When he reached home that evening and opened his room, he discovered the three kids of the lawyer huddled in a corner of the verandah. The grandmother had perhaps frightened them by telling stories about demons. The old man sat at a distance and chewed paan. However, Natabar made a new discovery that a cow had been tied to a post below the verandah. A newborn calf stood near the mango tree in an enclosure and lowed. Somehow it created the environment of a family. Unaccustomed to alcohol, Natabar turned emotional. He unlocked his room and sat on the bed. He looked at his body as he took off his shirt, somewhat taken aback. "This body is dying out gradually ... the major problem now is food – it's neither a dwelling place nor clothes ..." he said to himself.

He recalled his promise of the evening at that time – he had to dance naked.

He laughed to himself – like a drunk. Then he told himself – was he really going to dance with a physique like his? That too before a pregnant woman? Ha!" Suddenly, his stomach cramped with hunger. He didn't know what happened after that. Perhaps he slept peacefully after that because of the alcohol.

The fifth day passed amid total silence and some kind of introspection. He had neither gone to the college nor elsewhere that day.

On the day of the incident, a few enthusiastic youth of the street knocked on his door. There was a programme of a picketing in the municipal fish market. Meetings were held for a few days protesting against the increase in the price of fish in the market. The price of fish had suddenly galloped from three rupees to seven rupees a seer. Those enthusiastic young men of the street had passed certain resolutions for the picketing in a meeting held the previous evening.

Natabar was tired. His head seemed to be vacant and weightless. The young men entered his room at this time. Extending the paper carrying the resolutions of the previous night, they said, "Sir, you must come with us. The people of this street have also turned into dullards having lived with these dull professors for such a long time. They don't budge from their places whatever you do."

"These people understand nothing. They are not bothered even if ruin is staring them in the face," someone else was saying – close to Natabar's ears.

But Natabar continued to sleep, not bothered in the least. .

A couple of boys known to him pulled him by his arm and lifted him up.

"You may not join the picketing – but come and stand beside us. The importance of the matter will increase manifold if highly educated scientists like you show your solidarity with us. What do you say, Natabar Babu? Come on, get up!"

"My dear friend! He belongs to the field of chemistry.

If he speaks just a few words ... to inflame the crowd! Let him only say – how protein is vital for our body, how much vitamin we need ... how much protein and vitamin are available in one seer of fish and how much that would cost in the form of medicines – let him just provide some statistics ... you'll see how the crowd will start yelling for blood. The fishmongers would be left staring ...."

The weight of Natabar's head was increasing gradually and the hangover of the alcohol he had imbibed the previous evening was passing off. Hence, the inciting dosages administered by the young men had started to work inside his head by that time. He opened his eyes and looked around him –

He looked at each one's face. Each of them looked well fed – the cheeks were like well rounded apples! The complexion was like that of a ripe banana! They looked fresh like a basket of spinach. Shining like a basket of garden fresh black brinjals. Juicy like a basket of oranges! Betel juice was flowing down from the lips.

These people had started to reduce the price of fish.

Natabar smiled!

They looked bewildered –

"You're smiling! Do you think that the picketing would be of no use?"

"Why not?" Natabar continued to smile and said, "It would be successful. But science says that only proteins are not needed for a balanced meal. You'll bring about a reduction in the price of fish. Okay, but ...."

"Oh yes, Sir! That is also included in our agenda! You are talking about the paddy that is being smuggled out to West Bengal, aren't you? We know that rice costs two rupees a seer! We can stop it in a single night if we wish. We just have to keep a watch at the banks of Mahanadi ...."

"And Sir!" someone else joined in, "Paddy is going to the north – but truckloads of fertilizers are being sent to the south. And that fertilizer is coming for our farmers! But the same fertilizer is being siphoned off to the breweries."

"Oh, really?" It was news for Natabar. He had only read in the books that ammonium sulphate was needed to make alcohol. Was he behind the times?

"And sugar?" the first one continued again, "Sugar is not available in the market – the shopkeepers have hoarded everything – sugar is selling for two rupees and four annas per seer! Even that is adulterated with sand and ground glass!"

"And what about milk powder? Have you heard that fourteen children died in a school after drinking milk powder!"

"Fourteen?" Natabar seemed amazed. He asked again, "Fourteen school children died?"

"Aren't you reading the newspapers? Whither this country is going – and look at our people in the professors' colony! Ignorance is bliss indeed!" Someone poked Natabar in the waist.

Hundreds of people had died a few days back in Kerala and Calcutta by eating poisonous food made of flour. A rickshaw puller had died after eating wadaas in a hotel in Nimchouri. People were scared in Orissa after the newspapers carried the news that many people had suffered from paralysis after eating stuff made of flour.

All these seemed to assimilate inside the hungry stomach and parched throat of Natabar – like alcohol.

And it kept on raining ….

"Do you think that this is the end of it? There is more to come. My dear friend! The scriptures say –

'People would turn wicked,

They would destroy the earth ....'

It is again said –

'The north would be wrecked; the south will be inundated,

No one would be left alive in the east,

In the bushes ... eh, what's going to happen?

Yes, they would turn into seeds!'

What does it mean that only the people living in the jungles would find food to eat. Otherwise, who can continue to eat with meat selling at four or five rupees a seer and fish at seven rupees? Who has got that kind of money?"

But the interpretation of the scriptures was carried even deeper.

"Does 'north' mean that? North means Russia! Didn't you see? It dropped a fifty megaton atomic bomb and now blood would start raining from the skies – just wait and see. The newspapers say that many people are suffering there from cancer because of this!"

"It's not Russia, stupid – it's China! The way it had rushed inside India in 1956 and 1959 – you'll see! If it doesn't make your life miserable in another couple of years ...!"

"Aw! Forget about Russia and China! Think of Orissa now! Do you know? The Na'Anka Famine has now started in Balasore district of Orissa. Paddy is being carried to Calcutta through the sea route. Mark my word - if Orissa doesn't observe the centenary of the Na'Anka Famine ...! Already there is a clamour for rice!"

"Orissa – hundred years back and now! What's the difference! What difference does one Hirakud make? Floods occur as regularly now as before! The same goes for droughts! The factors that led to the Na'Anka Famine a hundred years back are there even today. The same smuggling of paddy ... non-availability of wagons ...."

"Alas! There were people near you those days to come to your aid. They responded when you called for help – the walking God of Orissa – Utkalmani and in a manner of speaking, his Pandava brothers … who's there today to listen to the pleas of the poor Oriyas?"

That was it!

Natabar sat up in a flash!

No – he would go with the procession. He would join the picketing before the fish stalls. He would go – he would go as the leader of the procession.

The features of a huge man flashed before his eyes. The man who barged into the band of striking students throwing caution to the wind the day he took admission in the college. He would barge into the crowd at the fish market the same way.

Leader of the people! A good leader of the people was needed in this age ….

Natabar marched in the front. He was followed by the enthusiastic young men. Someone was shouting a slogan – "Fish must sell for eight annas a seer."

"Down, down - profit seekers."

The procession proceeded from the fruit market towards the city.

Fruit market!

The Mediterranean climate prevailed here – at the heart of Orissa. There were loads of fruits on both sides of the road! Vegetables! It was beautiful!

Natabar licked his lips glancing at a basket of oranges.

Oh! How terrible that reaction was – inside the stomach!

The swollen-cheeked, enthusiastic young men were following him, "Fish must sell for eight annas a seer."

The fathers, brothers and uncles of these young men were smiling, looking at the procession.

This was new blood, new youth.

Natabar could not contain himself any longer. He slipped away quietly. He went to a shop selling oranges.

"Brother, how many oranges for a rupee?"

The shopkeeper was staring towards the procession. Absentmindedly, he answered, "Two!"

"Two? Just two? And what about that heap of rotten ones on that side?" Natabar said pointing his hand at a rotten orange.

The shopkeeper had a stick in his hand. Absentmindedly, he rapped him on the knuckles. The stick fell on that particular finger – the one which his village school teacher used to hit all the time. Natabar withdrew his hand.

His hunger had still not subsided. In stead of extending his hand at the bunch of bananas, he stood at a distance and asked, "Brother, how much for a dozen of bananas?"

"Twelve annas."

"Twelve annas? Each one anna?"

"One anna each."

Natabar was angry. Suddenly, he said, "Brother! All these people who are going in the procession are your sons or grandsons, no? The per capita income in India is just six annas! Out of the six annas, one anna goes for a lousy banana! Where is the money for fish?'

The man still didn't pay any heed to the useless arguments of Natabar. He was only brandishing the stick – as if he was warding off the flies.

Natabar turned and again reached the original place – in front of the procession.

Suddenly, he shouted, "Let a dozen of bananas sell for one paisa!"

The crowd could not distinguish between this slogan and the first one. Mechanically, it returned the call of Natabar, "Let a dozen of bananas sell for one paisa!"

Without gauging the reaction of the crowd, Natabar again shouted, "Let brinjals sell for two paise."

Suddenly, there was a murmur in the crowd. The enthusiastic young men didn't respond to his call. The young men looked at both sides of the road, bewildered.

Natabar was about to yell again when a lathi hit his head.

As he took a tumble, he saw that the lathi belonged to one of the enthusiastic young men – the one who had stimulated him a while ago by saying that the Na'Anka Famine had arrived again.

But there was no scope there to think of anything. The lathis had started swinging like the Sudarshana Chakra at that place.

Sudarsana Chakras followed wherever Natabar ran.

The people in the procession scattered in a flash. Someone entered a house, some others jumped into drains – all these were spectators.

The young men ran after them, lathis in hand.

One shaven headed boy ran inside the college premises to save his life. The young men mistook him to be Natabar and ran after him.

That boy running near the college playground that day in the afternoon was not Natabar.

Like a wise, careful leader of the people, Natabar saved himself from the lathis of the enthusiastic young men; but that swelling on his forehead – the first blow of the lathi – stayed for a long time.

* * * **

Bibhuprasad went in a rickshaw that evening. He

carried all belongings of Natabar from that mess in the Professors' Colony.

The lawyer was not at home.

For some reason, the three kids smiled upon seeing Bibhuprasad. Someone even called him from behind, "Uncle, uncle …."

"He's not your uncle, kids. He's someone else. Who are you calling as uncle?" someone was chastising them from inside the house.

EIGHT

'Niraba Nilaya', Bibhuprasad's mess, was renamed after Natabar came and stayed with him.

The history and situation of Bibhuprasad's residence was like this. This was the only place available to him in the entire city as a shelter – this one-roomed house with a tin roof – the day Bibhuprasad had to leave the post graduate hostel under a certain disconcerting situation. Bibhuprasad had no idea why anyone had built that house in such a forlorn area. But when he took the house on a rent of ten rupees per month from Prof. Nayak of the Department of Physics, the professor called him one day after all the formalities were completed and said, "Look! There would be a bit of trouble in the house in the beginning. I've bought it only recently. Some other people were interested in buying it. They might cause trouble. But don't you worry."

Bibhuprasad was somewhat worried on listening to such a warning immediately after moving in to the house. The professor could see Bibhuprasad's concern. Hence, he made matters simple and said, "See! Don't think there are ghosts or something there. But you have to remove a Gurkha from that place. That Gurkha works for the owner of the saw mill that is being set up on the other side. That man had his eye on this place. But I bought it from its Marwari owner. Naturally, the man is nursing a grudge against me. You just win over the Gurkha and make sure that he does not meddle."

The word Gurkha had only created a weird image in Bibhuprasad's mind. There was the image of someone flashing a bayonet and retracing his steps quickly to hide behind a bush.

Be that as it may, he finally managed to get rid of the Gurkha after keeping him in good humour for a month and paying a baksheesh of five rupees. And the day the house became unencumbered and Bibhuprasad put up a name plate on the door along with the words 'Niraba Nilaya', there was continuous pelting of stones on the tin roof that continued for seven days and seven nights. Then it stopped abruptly one day – just the way it had started. But the next day, Prof. Nayak's cook arrived with a letter and from that day onwards, the rent of the house was increased at the rate of two rupees per annum. It was nudging twenty rupees a month now. And it seemed to Bibhuprasad that the length, width and height of that small house had gone on decreasing gradually from that day. He also knew why. It was the relative reaction of all those saw mills, hume pipe depots, potato godowns, motor body building workshops, etc. around that house that had steadily gone on increasing in number.

In order to be a partner in the increased rent of 'Niraba Nilaya', Bibhuprasad brought Natabar that day to him.

A number of days had passed since the day picketing had been organized in front of the fruit shops. But that awkward swelling on Natabar's forehead had still not gone away. Perhaps it was not going to disappear ever.

In the meantime, a comet had started moving around in the research horizon of the college for some time. The discussions in the tea club had started hotting up and cornering all the ears. The discussions always started from that one point – the pay scales. Of course, the scales changed after that and the strings reached their limit when they could go up no further. The string should break after that with a metallic sound or some sound should be heard from the skies like dry thunder; but that did not happen. Hence, discussions stopped there with that one line – 'Dwarka would be destroyed because of a huge flood.'

Returning from tuition, Natabar ordered Bibhuprasad that evening –

"Look! The name plate of this mess will be changed from tomorrow. I've already placed the order. The new name plate would be – 'Pathology Laboratory – Stool and urine examined here'".

Bibhuprasad had just returned from the banks of Mahanadi at the time. Apart from that, he had received a letter that day through the manager of the Healthy Food Mart that the headmaster of the school where his father served was retiring. Hence, his father might be appointed as the headmaster of the school very soon. Bibhuprasad had kept the letter in his pocket. Tears had still not dried up from his eyes after reading that emotion-filled letter. So, the man was finally going to reach his coveted destination!

Natabar was angry when he found Bibhuprasad to be quiet and cold. He said, "I hate you for this reason, Bibhuprasad! You can't catch up with an idea. You know very well that this is the age of technology. And if you stay hungry in this age, then you are a sinner – you are dumb. The idea struck me today – it's a fantastic idea. What do you say?"

Bibhuprasad was still silent. That letter had kept his mind occupied. His father had written, "I don't know how forty years have passed even as I was scratching my ears …. My time is up too. Now I wonder – what have I got from these forty years? Someone is telling me silently at times –

you children were right! I would have at least enjoyed my life a little bit more because of the money if I had taken up that job in the police force ...."

But, in stead of giving him any further time to think, Natabar gave him a shove and tried to convince him, "Look! This is a highly profitable profession. Of course, we would not take this up as a business proposition. It should be taken up as a hobby – as a pastime. Look! Most of the people in this city would not be deprived of medical treatment if they could get the pathological investigations done somewhere. Just think for a moment – do all these rickshaw pullers, school kids, school teachers and the numerous other poor people around us have the capacity to pay four rupees every time they have to get their stool examined? If we open a laboratory here and examine stool at two rupees per head, won't we be doing a service to the nation?"

Bibhuprasad was thinking of that emotion-filled portion of the letter written by his father. He had written, "But I think about it again – what have I not seen in these thirty five years? If the meaning of life is to see, taste, hear and smell, then I've had enough of those. When I look at a potato even now, all its geographical thrills come floating before me. I can clearly see the foothills of the beautiful Andes! I can see the mouth of Amazon ...! The snow-capped peak of the Himalayas!

"When I look at your faces at times, I feel your problem is not malnutrition! What you lack is sensitivity to beauty. I am not a student of science; but I've heard – Sir Jagdish Chandra could apparently carry on a conversation with plants. He must have been able to do so; otherwise, which idiot could ever feel the sensitiveness of plants as long as the sun and the moon ...."

Natabar finally lost his patience without getting any

reply from Bibhuprasad. What followed after that was but natural. Bibhuprasad finally took an interest in what Natabar was saying.

Natabar again explained his valuable idea from the beginning. He said, "Look! The application of science is more important than science per se now, especially in an underdeveloped country like ours. Look at yourself! Okay, what have we achieved by way of research? We have only done some novel imitation in the name of original research. If there is research on diesel, cottonseed oil or groundnut oil in America, we do research on cassia oil here. But what would be the final outcome? America would supply rice to us and we would produce dozens of paper Ph.D.s eating that rice! When America would be lifting millions of dollars from this country, the researchers and professors of this country would be running from the office of the Director of Public Instruction to the Secretariat for two increments. And that money would also not reach them in the end. There would be people like Manmohan in the middle to block that!"

"So, what do you want to say?" Bibhuprasad finally opened his mouth. He argued, "Do you mean to say that there should not be any research here? We would be looking at the scientists of America only! There won't be any research on drugs here. What's going to happen if there is a war between India and America?"

"If there is a war with America …? You would be annihilated first … do you have hydrogen bombs with you??"

"In that case, we should first make hydrogen bombs …." Bibhuprasad teased.

Natabar said from between his clenched teeth, "Idiot! Do you think hydrogen bombs are made from thin air? One who doesn't have money to get his stool examined wants to make hydrogen bombs!"

Bibhuprasad smiled a bit staring at Natabar's face – then he gave him the right answer. He said, "And do you mean to say that examination of stool shall be made just like that? When one doesn't have food in the stomach, where would you get the stool to examine?"

Natabar fell quiet for a while. Then he dismissed all Bibhuprasad's arguments with a wave of his hand. He said, "But the signboard will definitely be hung here from tomorrow, you'll see. You don't need to worry. I'll take care of everything. Let stool form in the stomach first!"

Bibhuprasad could understand the meaning of all these arguments of Natabar. There was no doubt that all these were the reactions to the assault on him at the time of that picketing.

Discussions continued after that throughout the night. Natabar seldom discussed women. Women and slumber – like any great man of the world, these two reminded him of that one outcome – the final outcome of the mortal human body.

But Murasha somehow crept into the conversation. Of course, she did not come on her own. Bibhuprasad dragged her. In order to tease Natabar, he said, "I don't know why …. But perhaps she wants to meet me alone at times. Do you know? She often comes to the laboratory on some pretext or other when none of you is around. But what does she really want?"

Natabar did not reply.

Bibhuprasad again said, "Tell me one thing! Is she really making an effort to find a job as an air hostess or is she taking us for a ride? But she is not all that beautiful – to fit the bill as an air hostess! I think no one can be an air hostess easily if she is not as beautiful as a cine star! This is the age of cinema. Apart from that, one needs a lot of influence to enter into company service. Can Murasha succeed?"

Natabar feigned sleep. Of course, he had stared in the dark thinking about something.

However, unable to hide his emotions, Bibhuprasad blurted out, "Do you know? I have a great weakness for that girl. When I saw her near that jasmine plant outside the library for the first time – did you know? She comes from a place near my village – I got the information later when I enquired."

Natabar stirred and located Bibhuprasad's face in the dim light of the lantern. Then he said, "Stay within limits, Bibhuprasad! Don't bluff so much, I'm telling you. You should know that I know her a great deal more even before you got acquainted with her. She doesn't come from a place near your village either. Apart from everything else, you do not know her at all."

Of course, it was not possible to see any change of expression on Bibhuprasad's face in that dim light. But he smiled slightly and said, "There is a great deal of pleasure in not knowing her at all, brother! I may not know her – so what? But I can see that lighted wick that she is holding in her hand – and I can stand in an ice cold pond looking at that – on a winter night! She is my inspiration! My life! My everything!"

"Inspiration, my foot! For all you know, Manmohan might put her in the family way while arranging the letter of recommendation!" the intolerant voice of Natabar was quite apparent.

"Be careful!" Bibhuprasad was suddenly angry, "Don't spread rumours against a lady like an uncivilized person! That's a sin! We've no idea – with what hopes and aspirations, the poor girl is trying to make something of her, and that too to become an air hostess! Mark that indomitable desire of hers to fly. And her sister – that poor nurse! Poor girl! Oh no!" Bibhuprasad heaved a deep sigh.

Natabar was quiet.

Bibhuprasad too remained quiet for a while.

Bibhuprasad started talking again. He said, "Better give this idea of pathological investigations to Murasha's sister. She is a nurse. She knows about these things and she would be interested in this kind of work. Pass on the ideas to someone who would be able to do something about them rather than meddling yourself in those things."

"Keep quiet!" Natabar turned his face to the other side and said, "Helping others is passé. Those things are gone with the days of the feudalists. You would be beaten up if you talk about such things …."

Natabar slept.

Bibhuprasad thought of several things till late at night with his eyes closed – starting from that pen friend Lucy to the hypnotic charm received from Dr. V.K.S.D.N. Naidu.

Lucy! Bibhuprasad recalled – those were his childhood days! No! Lucy was just not a girl – this Lucy! She was always there in Bibhuprasad's mind – the first word in that letter carrying the postage mark of Philadelphia was 'Darling!' She still lived in the music of this most wonderful greeting.

He was studying in class nine at the time. That was the time and age to create pen friends. The way advertisements appear in newspapers these days – 'Pass M.A. while sitting at home' – sensational advertisements appeared those days in the shape of 'Make friends with people of the seven continents while sitting at home'. This had caught the fancies of many students including Bibhuprasad and as a consequence, Bibhuprasad had got that pen friend of his – Lucy.

But the circumstances under which that sweet, nodding acquaintance with Lucy had to be terminated – Bibhuprasad laughed as much as he was saddened when he thought about the event sometime now. And he got angry with the inclination of his father to unnecessarily act as the schoolmaster even when the circumstances did not warrant it.

Bhabaniprasad discovered that letter that day as he was rummaging through Bibhuprasad's suitcase for some reason.

That such a contraband item could ever be discovered suddenly in the box of a class nine boy – Bhabaniprasad could not perhaps believe his own eyes.

Bibhuprasad still remembered – his father roared while putting that question to him –

"Rascal! Tell me! Who's that girl?" A group of boys from the hostel gathered upon hearing him roar like that. The superintendent came. Writing of letters was stopped. But the most painful thing was – Bibhuprasad discovered Lucy corresponding with another boy from his class later. The unnatural death of Lucy that occurred amid several rounds of discussions and criticisms – the mark of that wound had not been effaced for as long as he had lived, nor was it likely to be ever effaced.

And, now after a long time – Murasha stood as the symbol of that suffering – before Bibhuprasad.

Yes! This was that Murasha – in order to win over whom Bibhuprasad had one day felt the need for a hypnotic charm!

Bibhuprasad had first discovered Murasha there –

where he had stood for the first time in the shade of that flower plant under the high, multicoloured, royal windows of the Greek pagoda structured library and got acquainted with this great institution. Where those words of his father had taken him to the heaven of his hopes and aspirations in a flash and again worn him out under that large mass of water before he could bat an eyelid.

About seven years after this event – when Bibhuprasad had in fact risen to the heaven of his aspirations and had been an applicant for research scholarship having already got a hold on science – he discovered this unknown girl among a group of students who had just taken admission in the college! Later, he came to know that her name was Murasha!

Two rows of gorgeous balsam shrubs had stretched that day from the library to the portico where Muchukunda bloomed! Plenty of Muchukunda – at the foot of which two cannons from ancient times had been lying with their nozzles pointing up – sitting on top of which Manmohan narrated the story of his ancestors – which started as – "That was the time of the Na'Anka Famine! Ravenshaw Sahib was the Commissioner and my great, great grandfather ...."

A girl started out from this place, from this library. There was a load of books and a dissection box in her hand. The college had almost closed by then or perhaps the last period was in progress. The quadrangle was almost empty.

Manmohan, Natabar, Bibhuprasad and Mr. Sethi too – all of them were going to have their tea. They were still invisible in the shade of the flower plant outside the library.

Suddenly, Bibhuprasad noticed that the girl bent and picked up a flower. Manmohan and the others had not seen the girl until then. They were still engrossed in departmental politics – the conflicts between Dr. Jena and

Dr. Sharma. Manmohan was a supporter of Dr. Jena at the time and was getting into the habit of wearing a pair of cracked chappals and 'terykhaddar' clothes, since he had just started his research work. In order to frighten Mr. Sethi, who was Dr. Jena's student, he said, "I'll tell my father today. This Sharma fellow ought to be dispatched as the Principal of a lower primary school. The man is poisoning the entire atmosphere. I hear that the first divisions will be auctioned in this college this year. The government must be made aware of all these things!"

Bibhuprasad noticed – the girl looked from one side to the other again and lifted her hand to place that flower on her plait. Manmohan's laughter shattered the silence of the quadrangle at that time.

After that –

In the meanwhile, the girl tried to put together the scissors, scalpel, razor and needle, and tried to pick her dissection box and books up. But every time she tried to pick them up, they slipped out of her hands. Finally, the girl of course succeeded in picking everything up; but as Bibhuprasad walked with his friends towards the coffee shop, his gaze was fixed on the flower that was lying on the ground.

Bibhuprasad allowed his friends to walk on and picked up the flower in a flash when no one was looking. Then he hid it inside his pocket. Then he noticed – how the girl walked fast and tried to lose herself by the side of the two cannons near the portico.

A little while later – as they were sipping coffee – unable to hide his emotions any further, Bibhuprasad said –

"How I wished I could run to the girl and help her out – to pick up those books lying on the ground."

Natabar and Manmohan broke into smiles over their coffee cups and Natabar said –

"Oh dear! Blue lily and the Kathachampa!"

In order to defend himself, Bibhuprasad said, "You'll see! She will be the college queen this year! Why, I can't see a better girl than her!"

"How many girls have you seen in your life, you idiot?" Manmohan dismissed the matter lightly – in a manner that came naturally to him.

Observing the attack on Bibhuprasad, Mr. Sethi tried to come to his rescue and said hesitantly, "She is slightly dark; but she has grace."

Bibhuprasad said, "None of you has taken notice of that grace of hers – did you see her when she picked up that flower from the ground and was about to place it on her plait?"

In order to prove his point, Bibhuprasad pulled that flower from inside his pocket and extended it to Manmohan.

After that – the flower moved from one hand to another a number of times around that intoxicated coffee table. Each of them examined it, made some comment, put it to the nose and turned it around with the fingertips and then passed it on to the next man – just like a chillum filled with ganja.

A few days after the incident, Bibhuprasad heard that name from the mouth of Manmohan – Murasha!

Bibhuprasad was startled – no one knew why! And, immediately after that, Bibhuprasad needed to indulge in that courageous act – using the hypnotic charm of Dr. V.K.S.D.N. Naidu!

The story of Dr.V.K.S.D.N. Naidu was like this –

When Bibhuprasad moved into that one-room house in the beginning – the Gurkha had left and the pelting of stones had stopped from the direction of the saw mill since a few days – this V.K.S.D.N. fellow and his wife worked together at the time on several tin plates and put up a cabin by the side of the road. Of course, the man was still to assume the title of 'Dr.' at the time.

The man actually worked as a points man in the Railways some time back. He was dismissed from service after he lost an eye in a railway accident and he set up a cabin in that lonely spot. The husband and wife were busy in all kinds of odd jobs around the hut all day long – Bibhuprasad called them the squirrel and the sparrow!

One day – Bibhuprasad found ten to fifteen rickshaws gathering around the hut and he also saw that a tin plate had been affixed to the trunk of the huge tree near the hut. That name had been written on that tin plate in English and some other language – probably Telugu –

"DR. V.K.S.D.N.NAIDU"

Bibhuprasad also noticed another tin plate at another place on the trunk of that tree. He could not read it; but he managed to gather its gist later. The writing conveyed the following to the reader –

"Brothers and sisters! Donate blood for the country and the community!"

Until then, Bibhuprasad had thought that it was a government advertisement since blood donation had assumed the shape of a movement at the time throughout the country. New blood banks were opening everywhere. People, especially rickshaw pullers, thronged such places to sell their blood.

Very few people were aware at the time that it was a highly profitable business to gather the rickshaw pullers of the city in a peaceful and organized manner and take them to blood banks on specified days with an eye on their health. Besides, very few people had caught on to the idea that cheap medicines for scabbies and stomach aches, the two major diseases rickshaw pullers suffered from, could be easily sold through such an agency.

By evening, a battalion of patients had arrived at the place of those two – the squirrel and the sparrow. During the course of a night, Dr. Naidu had turned into Dr. Albert Schweitzer, the Nobel Prize winning doctor of the African jungle!

And a year passed in this manner.

One day, Dr. Naidu suddenly arrived at Bibhuprasad's place. Bibhuprasad had the opportunity to talk to the man for the first time that day.

Looking at the eye that had survived the train accident, Bibhuprasad could notice that a great life force worked there, inside it. That eye compelled him to listen to the man.

"Would you please keep this box at your place for a while?" the man requested Bibhuprasad.

Without wasting any words, Bibhuprasad kept the small suitcase the man had brought along with him.

The man left. At midnight, Bibhuprasad heard some noise and saw that Dr. Naidu's house was being searched. A few policemen had surrounded the house, rifles slung across their shoulders.

The police left by the morning. Dr. Naidu arrived at Bibhuprasad's house the next day. The man looked calm and quiet as on any other day. Exactly like a squirrel!

The man took the box from Bibhuprasad. He said, "You helped me when I was in trouble. Tell me – what can I do for you?"

Bibhuprasad could say nothing.

The man examined the sad face of the boy for a while

and said with a smile, "Me and my wife have kept an eye on you for the past few days. Why, we've never seen you smile! My wife also says the same thing."

Bibhuprasad felt a bit uncomfortable with the remark.

"What worries you all the time?" the man again seemed to be making an accusation, "Woman? Don't you want a woman … in that lonely house of yours … means, just for the sake of …!"

Then the man pushed near him and whispered in his ear, "You see! I would definitely help you since you've done me a favour."

The man was standing – at the doorstep. Bibhuprasad noticed the darkness outside.

"You see! You're a trustworthy person. There's stuff worth more than one lakh rupees inside this box. I can see from the seal that you haven't touched anything. We've orders to help trustworthy people like you. Take this charm – order it anything and all your wishes will come true. This is the order of Goddess Kamakshi of Assam. Do not disbelieve what I am saying."

The man vanished in the darkness of the night – with his box. Bibhuprasad was feeling a shiver run down him. The night passed and the morning came. The charm was still on the table where the man had left it.

And this was the same charm that Bibhuprasad had tied to his arm now and set out to test its properties – on that girl called Murasha.

But alas!

He was Bibhuprasad indeed – for whom the charm had been meant. When he tied the charm to his arm and followed a girl for the first time in his life, some outside force seemed to have put his voice box out of order. It seemed he had lost himself at some point in time. Someone seemed to have gripped his throat all of a sudden – inside an iron fist. Oh no!

Bibhuprasad could not steal Murasha that day from the clutches of Manmohan. Finally, he threw the charm into the Mahanadi that evening where Natabar had one day cast his father's cap! That camel-haired cap!

That hut was no longer there. The double-storied building of a contractor stood there now. A bird's cage hung from the balcony of that house. An old parrot from that cage is sometimes called "Radha! Radha!" The elderly contractor stood there at times gazing at the mango tree, lost to the world around him.

Bibhuprasad was sometime startled to see that cage and the elderly contractor in that state. He felt as if that Dr.V.K.S.D.N. Naidu stood there watching him. And the cage was actually that charm that Bibhuprasad had cast into the river that day out of fear.

NINE

The signboard proclaiming, "Pathology Laboratory" had been put up in the meantime below the signboard "Niraba Nilaya". Bibhuprasad was opposed to it; Natabar was all for it. Finally, the signboard was put up. Large letters on a huge black board that glittered even from a distance.

However, Bibhuprasad was reassured on one count. Natabar had not started any work even though the sign board had been put up. He was busy undergoing training at the time. A doctor-friend gave him training in a hospital. He had almost stopped going to college these days. He was totally focused on that one fad of his. He would be a businessman. He would start that future project of his by rendering service to the nation through pathological investigations.

A paper submitted by Bibhuprasad a long time back had been published in the meantime – in a reputed journal. A professor from some foreign university had written a letter praising it profusely and had requested for a reprint. The letter had come to Dr. Jena.

Prof. Jena called Bibhuprasad and handed over the letter to him that day. Pointing at the letter, he said, "Do you see? They have already prefixed your name with the word 'Dr.'. What do you say? You're happy now, no?"

Bibhuprasad looked towards Dr. Jena. He smiled for a moment with a great sense of achievement. But he got a hold of himself the next moment. For some reason, his eyes turned moist.

Then they talked about several things. About Natabar, about Manmohan, about research in general and so forth.

Manmohan too has not come to the laboratory for the past few days. Dr. Jena knew that he was trying to go to Germany at the time. He was busy with that. He was likely to go to Calcutta one of these days for his visa.

Several topics came up for discussion when they talked about foreign universities. Dr. Jena recalled his experiences and narrated the mode of research in those countries. He talked about their laboratories, researchers, education system, professors, the importance attached to education, the place of professors in society and so forth. He also narrated how the sahibs used to look down upon our language and called it 'native'. He also maintained that the Ph.D.s produced in our laboratories were still branded as 'native' and treated with disdain.

After that, Dr. Jena encouraged Bibhuprasad again and said, "But do you see how things have changed now? The same professors have now started praising our 'native' papers. Keep this! Keep this with you! This is your ultimate certificate. This is your glory!"

"No, Sir! Bibhuprasad expressed his gratitude in an extremely humble voice, "This is indeed your glory and the glory of my nation. Not mine!"

Then he talked about Natabar. Prof. Jena said sadly, "The poor boy has gone astray. He is a sharp and brilliant student. I had an idea …. Oh, forget it! But I know. This country will not permit a brilliant boy like him to concentrate on science. They would always pull him towards politics."

Prof. Jena had already heard of Natabar's misadventures in front of the fruit stall. Alluding to that incident, he said, "You'll see! If this fellow doesn't turn into a communist some day! The path that he has chosen …."

Bibhuprasad was lost in thought for a while. Then he thought of some thing and said, "Not a communist, Sir! He will turn out to be a pucca Nazi. Just as Hitler had been born out of the persecution of the Jews …!"

Dr. Jena changed the topic. Then he got up to go. Before leaving, he said, "I believe you need to extract some more cassia oil for the third leg of your research. You do that today. Make some more cassia oil."

Bibhuprasad went to the tea club of the college some time later. Harish, the old man, came to greet him. He placed a cup of tea before him, caressed him on the back and said, "Well done! Well done! I am told that you have published a wonderful paper. More sugar?"

Bibhuprasad turned empathic towards the old man looking at his white moustache and the pumpkin-shaped face.

Of course, the matter was first raised by the old man. He said, "Why Sir! Would this boy go astray even when all of you are around?"

"Which boy? Bibhuprasad asked, a bit taken aback.

"Why? That Natabar chap! Such a wonderful boy! What self-confidence he has! A devil-may-care gait! I remember it still. One day, he was saying, 'Just wait for a while. If I don't win the Nobel Prize!' How he talked! How he carried himself! But he has gone astray – you are his friends and you don't seem to be doing anything for him!"

Bibhuprasad concentrated on sipping tea. He was thinking – Harish's daughter would pass Pre-University this year. Her name was Malati; but old man Harish, the peon of the Chemistry Department, was also no less romantic – just like his father Bhawaniprasad! Just as he could see the foothills of the Andes mountain range upon looking at a potato – old man Harish could similarly feel the inspiration behind the poem of Sir Ramsay glancing at that thin, shapeless daughter of his. Harish had given a nickname to the girl – Hili! That nickname Hili was like the miniscule quantity of extremely light gas called helium in the atmosphere. The day Sir Ramsay would have felt the existence of this most invisible gas of this invisible atmosphere – he would have addressed the gas just as affectionately – Hili!

Some arguments could be heard from inside the tea club at this time. Bibhuprasad listened. He thought that a discussion must be going on about the pay scale since the Pay Commission Report had already been made public or was about to be made public. Manmohan had informed everyone in advance that there was a provision to increase the salary of college teachers in that report. There was excitement among service holders everywhere in Orissa because of the news. People could be seen everywhere with a pencil, a long piece of paper and a calculator in hand.

But Bibhuprasad felt an electric shock going through him – when Harish returned from somewhere and said with a contorted face, "Oh, no! Oh, no! Both the kids passed away! Who can console the father!"

And, in a moment, Bibhuprasad knew who the father was. He had heard that the two children of Mr. Sethi had been ill for the last few days. Mr. Sethi was saying that the children were suffering. Both of them returned from school one day and went to bed. They had loose motion and vomiting. They showed some signs of improvement after a great deal of treatment. But something happened thereafter – the eyes of one were dilated and the face of the other was pulled to one side. So … the children passed away finally?

Bibhuprasad himself felt terribly ill for some reason upon hearing the news. He even vomited for a little while. He kept recalling that smell – the smell of that cooking oil pot that had hit his nose when he was having his lunch earlier in the day at the Healthy Food Mart. Who knew what it might have been adulterated with?

Bibhuprasad vomited yet again. He was caressing his own face without being aware of it – as if some terrible apprehension was working on his subconscious. He was examining the muscles on his face repeatedly to make sure that everything was in place.

X XX X X X

Natabar returned home late that day after finishing his training and tuition.

It was getting to be quite hot. It was perhaps the later part of March. A swift breeze was blowing outside. Bibhuprasad had pulled a charpoy outside and been lying on it. The light of the moon caressed his eyes. But the electric bulbs burning around the house hurt his eyes. One could not perhaps feel that other light until one became very conscious of the moon.

But Bibhuprasad was not looking at the moon at the time. His gaze was slowly returning from the moon towards that mango tree beyond the boundary wall. The mango tree was not visible clearly in the night; but its dark shape created an image. Bibhuprasad thought of the mango tree in his village. It would be laced all over with mangoes by now. A few might already have ripened.

Bibhuprasad was thinking. His eyes again moved from that mango tree – towards that house. The house of the contractor and the chanting of the old parrot – Radha! Radha!

Bibhuprasad looked at the contractor's house. A few rays of light fell from the tube light inside the house on the porch. A few people were moving around there.

A cow suddenly started lowing. The lowing sound of the cow along with the buzz coming from the refrigerator of the potato godown and the nearby saw mill – all these blended to create a music of its own.

Bibhuprasad recalled the days – when he suffered repeatedly from malaria in his childhood – there was fever followed by bouts of rigor – someone covered him up with a blanket – Bibhuprasad could not keep track of things after that – but when he heard the lowing of cows going out to graze after a while – the sound of the engines of buses plying on the distant highway – he pricked his ears inside the blanket – nothing made sense to him at the time – numerous light points surrounded his eyes for a long time from inside the tiny holes in the blanket – for some reason, a little bit of excitement ran through his weak mind some time later – the warning bell of the village school rang in the distance – of course, he did not read in the school at the time; but somehow he felt good. He was aware that the time to leave for the school had passed, and perhaps, he might go towards the mango grove when the afternoon came.

Bibhuprasad came back to his senses. But his mind returned to that house again. No, towards the owner of the house

Once upon a time, he was a lowly employee in the agriculture department. The poor fellow worked as a mere clerk. Oh, no! Life must have been really hard for him. He too might have lost his kids – one, two, three, four … out of hunger or because of poisoned food stuff. But what happened? There – over there – a motor garage is building up. He has forty trucks running on the highways all the time. They returned at intervals. They gathered in the garage. Work went on throughout the night. By morning, they were again ready to do their bidding – those one hundred and sixty wheels of those forty trucks – nay, two hundred and forty wheels.

But how? How was it possible …?

Bibhuprasad kept staring at that house. And he could hear that lowing – the lowing of a cow.

Natabar barged in like a tornado at this time – from inside that darkness. He started speaking before Bibhuprasad could even see his face, "Bibhu! I've hit upon a wonderful idea. Listen to me!"

When he heard the excited voice of Natabar, Bibhuprasad felt that he was actually suffering from malaria and that herd of cows was on its way to graze outside followed by that cowherd – whose name was Judhesti, the mad one; but that sound of the wonderful, live voice … ghreeeee … ho …ooooo!!!

Natabar sat down on the bed of Natabar and said excitedly, "I had no idea that a chemical industry could be started so easily; but I heard today from someone … do you know, Bibhuprasad? You've no idea how easily mohar salt, i.e. ferrous ammonium sulphate could be produced! Look! These dry batteries … the batteries used in torch lights and radios which we throw away after use … if we could just pick them up! Some scrap iron is all that we need beside these. And a bit of sulphuric acid! Ferrous ammonium sulphate sells for eleven rupees and eight annas a bottle in the market …. What do you say? Shall we start?"

Bibhuprasad remained quiet.

"Believe me, brother! I've got this information from a pucca businessman. And he is the kind of man who belongs to a community which is famous throughout India for its business acumen. He has also told me – the formula for getting dry batteries! Do you know? Maunds of exhausted dry batteries are auctioned by the Railways at the Khurda Road station every six months!"

Bibhuprasad was still quiet.

Natabar waited for his answer; but he got angry like every other day when Natabar started yawning and said suddenly, "Look! This is what I am going to do if you don't encourage me this time too …."

And Bibhuprasad could feel in that faint light of the moon – that hand dangling near his neck – the hand of Natabar!

Bibhuprasad was not scared. Of course, a few hairs on his body stood on their ends. He kept quiet even then. He started speaking after a little while, and asked in a hesitant voice, "Okay! How far has your plan regarding the pathological laboratory progressed?"

Natabar, however, answered in a very clear voice, "Can you lend me about seven to eight hundred rupees? I've to buy a microscope in the least – for the examination of stool and urine!"

"Did you not know about it earlier?" Bibhuprasad asked.

"I knew it all right. But …." Natabar fell silent as if he was confused for a while but said suddenly, "But, that is why I'm saying – we've to start further from the beginning in order to create capital – that means I've to start now from the dry batteries that are being thrown away."

Bibhuprasad smiled now and said, "Was I not telling you the same thing? Everything in this country needs to be done again from the beginning."

The two friends were silent for a few minutes after that. Bibhuprasad declared after some time, "Look! I don't like this dry life any longer. I am going to say good bye to this research. I'm thinking of returning to the village where I would start afresh there. I'll keep a few chickens. I'll keep a cow. We've not been able to feel the warmth of any live thing – if we could maintain a relationship with something like a pet cat or even a silkworm!"

Natabar remained quiet. Perhaps he was suddenly sympathetic towards Bibhuprasad.

The two friends continued to sleep near each other till late at night after that, amid that total silence. Both were lying with their eyes closed. Each was lost in his own world.

Bibhuprasad wondered – how did that poor Dr. Jena live! He was lonely throughout his life – all alone. What did he think? What did he do? And what was he going to do – if Bibhuprasad gave up his research work?

Bibhuprasad recalled – he had also done that once in an angry moment some time back. He had stayed away from the laboratory for two to three days to take stock of his situation. Finally, he had written a letter like this to his father, "Father! I've decided to give up research after a great deal of deliberation. I can see that this kind of research cannot satisfy the hunger of my stomach and mind.

"I saw two states of gathering some knowledge about a matter by seeing the matter with my eyes. The first one was when I was an elephant and the matter before me was an ant; but now the matter before my eyes has grown so big that it has turned into an elephant and my eyes have turned into the eyes of an ant. I'm no longer able to see the matter; I can see only one of its atoms! I feel as if I've gone blind. Please save me from this 'specialization'. I am on my way to look for a job!"

Bibhuprasad received the answer to his letter after a couple of days from his father. It was the letter sent by him – sent back by post. Bibhuprasad was ashamed to see that there were some basic spelling mistakes in spite of all the care he had taken in drafting the letter which had been underlined with red ink as usual.

Of course, he himself arrived at his house the next day – his father. A prolonged argument started again between the father and the son; but his father triumphed at the end as usual. Bhabaniprasad was used from the beginning to find remedies for those temporary weakening of his son! He could understand everything instinctively by just looking at the face of his son. It was not unknown to him that Manmohan and his challenge for the Nobel Prize were behind the fatigue of Bibhuprasad.

Bhabaniprasad very improbably lost the arguments that had gone on throughout that day between the father and the son – that F.A. failed Assistant Head Master of an M.E. school, Bhabaniprasad.

But there was an unnatural change in the situation by that evening and it was seen that a father and son had been walking on that road to the west of the college, one following the other. The father in front and the son at the back. They were returning at the time from the residence of Prof. Jena by the side of the canal.

Bhabaniprasad exhorted his son to walk straight in his usual grave voice and said, "There was a Brahmin establishment on the sea shore ...."

Bibhuprasad surreptitiously took out a handkerchief from his pocket and wiped his moist eyes. And, suddenly, his slanted frame became straight without him being aware of it, and he listened attentively to the most favourite story of his father – which, of course, he had heard a number of times earlier. However, the story took such a new shape every time in a wholly new and unexpected circumstance that Bibhuprasad was always totally engrossed in it, and it took him a long time to discover himself again after losing himself in a vast expanse of greenery.

Yes! That was a scene of Chilika – a forgotten legend relating to a small island called Parikud located in the middle of the Chilika Lake.

Bhabaniprasad was too far gone by that time.

He continued, "It was the house of a Brahmin. The new daughter-in-law of the family wanted to defecate in the dead of the night. The poor girl called everyone in a low voice – she called her mother-in-law and sister-in-law. But who bothers about someone calling when sleep held complete sway!

"When no one responded, the poor girl did not know what to do and groped in the dark. She finally discovered a large pit in the north-east corner – it was the pit to receive the fire for an oblation! When the mother-in-law put her hand inside the ashes in the pit in the morning – Hallelujah! A beautiful cake of gold was found there. How did it get there? How did it get there? Someone finally found the answer – it was the faeces of the daughter-in-law.

"The mother-in-law called the daughter-in-law again the next day and made her sit on the pit. She stood guard beside her. Yet another solid cake of gold!

"Now look at the deeds of the mother-in-law! Her only work now was to make the daughter-in-law sit on the pit every morning and evening to defecate. Ornaments were made from gold. A new building was constructed – a house of gold. The hut disappeared into oblivion.

"How long could such a matter remain secret? The news spread that the faeces turned into gold the moment the daughter-in-law sat on the holy pit. Oh, no! Is that all?

Damn it! Were we all blind? How could we not see such a simple thing!

"The fire pits all over the village were filled with cakes of gold before dawn the next day! The entire village turned into Indra's palace. The houses of gold had gone on stretching towards the skies.

"An old Brahmin and his old wife lived on the edge of the village. One day, the old woman told the old man, 'Everyone became rich in the village. This village is full of gold, silver and diamonds. Can't you see anything? Shouldn't we get rich too? Why don't you ask me once – let me sit on your fire pit! You'll see if I haven't given you a cake of gold by tomorrow morning …!'

"The poor Brahmin didn't say anything to the old woman. He only glared at her and went on his way to beg. The next day, the old woman was again after the old man. But the Brahmin paid no heed. He glared at her again and left on his daily chore.

"It was the third day. Nothing was sacrosanct the third time. What happened next? When the old woman again quarreled with the Brahmin – the Brahmin could not contain himself any longer. Looking at the old woman with loving eyes, the Brahmin said, "Hey! Are you asking me for the last three days to destroy this beautiful place? Listen to me, you stupid old woman! Do you know why this place is still there in one piece? Do you have any idea about the foundation on which all these skyscrapers are standing? Listen to me! This place is still in existence because of this one undefiled fire pit! But the day you defile this one too – the foundation of this entire village will quake. It won't take a moment for this village of gold to be razed to earth!'

"'Oh, really? Do you have such power in you? What a pity … we don't get enough to eat even when my husband has such power in him! What could I do? Why don't I drop dead?'

"The Brahmin went out of his mind with the sarcasm of the old woman. Then he stood up. He pulled the old woman by her hand to take her outside the hut.

"And at exactly the same moment, the sea too started to rise – the ever faithful dog of truth!

"The old man and the old woman were walking – crossing those palaces of gold, crossing the township – far, far away …. The sea was following them – like a faithful dog true to its masters.

"After that ….

"The old man sat down under a banyan tree, exhausted. It was a dense tree. The roots of thousands of years had been buried in the earth. He took the bag off his shoulder and proceeded to make a platform for *homa*. There – under that huge tree.

"The huge mass of water was just behind him! The same thing! It was the same all around him. The old woman had been staring. She could see nothing else. Only water and water! The sea had stood waiting exactly like the faithful dog. This was the creation of Parikud! The legend of Chilika!"

The father and son returned from the residence of Dr. Jena, rubbing the eyes with the handkerchiefs. Bibhuprasad could not leave research – nor could research leave Bibhuprasad.

The two held each other intimately.

TEN

Loads of scraps of a variety of metals started gathering now around Bibhuprasad's 'Niraba Nilaya' and the proposed pathology laboratory of Natabar. For a week, Natabar was busy collecting the necessary materials for his newly proposed chemical cottage industry. Of course, it was not very difficult to collect these materials. If a tip of one or two rupees was given to the sweeper coming to clean the toilets of the contractor's house, he would find enough metal scrap from the municipality dust bin to keep his industry going for ever.

The scrap had arrived. It was the turn of old batteries of torch lights. Of course, it was slightly more difficult to collect these. Natabar tried to get the relevant information from Khurda Road by corresponding with the Railways; but he had very little control over the auctions conducted by the Railways. To his dismay, Natabar discovered that it was not as easy as he had thought to get the batteries through auction from the Railways. The reason was – an auction meant an auction! In other words, it meant competition. And competition meant money – finance! It was not all that easy to snatch the load of dry batteries of the Railways from the mouths of those traders who participated in these auctions earlier on a regular basis. Hence, Natabar had to depend again on that dust bin to collect raw material like dry batteries. 'Start from nothing!' It meant starting from scratch.

So, the major work of Natabar now was to use all his spare time in looking for batteries of torch lights from junk yards. Junk yard to junk yard – dust bin to dust bin – Natabar had been making the rounds.

And Bibhuprasad –

Of course, he had not been able to leave his 'Niraba Nilaya' in spite of all this madness of Natabar. Where could he go? Where was another place for him in that finite creation of the city of Cuttack? And how could he leave that house which was so full of memories – which he considered to be his very own! He was as sentimental and possessive about the house as an old family of farmers would be about their farm land. But why? Wasn't this 'Niraba Nilaya' once full of ant hills, scorpions and spiders – where he coexisted with a dangerous Gurkha one day? And where did he have to put up with the stone-pelting of seven spectral nights in order to assert his rights over the house? Was this not the same house 'Niraba Nilaya'? Bibhuprasad's very own?

Hence, Bibhuprasad was busy in his research work in spite of living in the increasing circumference of metal scrap and torch light batteries. Like every other day, he got up early in the morning, finished his daily chores and left for work – for the laboratory. Natabar was usually asleep at the time. But Natabar returned a bit late in the night. And Bibhuprasad took advantage of the situation to pull the charpoy outside and pass off to sleep. Thus, there was very little scope for any kind of conversation with Natabar the last few days.

However, Bibhuprasad was not too sure about the situation in the laboratory in spite of all this difficult coexistence and singlemindedness.

Another kind of rumour had started spreading in the tea club after the death of the two kids of Mr. Sethi. It was rumoured that Manmohan was returning again. For some reason, his foreign trip had been held up; but several stories were being heard about Manmohan's return. It was heard that he would not return as the student of Dr. Jena this time if he returned at all. He would return to the side of Dr. Sharma. And whenever two persons got together in the Department, the major topic of discussion at the time was to explore the implications of Manmohan returning to Dr. Sharma's side.

All these rumours reached Bibhuprasad's ears naturally. As much as he tried to ignore them, it was not possible on his part to do so. How could he do it? They were entangled with their own fate! More so, when everyone was eager today to resolve that fate – from peons to high-powered officials of the government.

Even as Bibhuprasad suffered in this manner, Dr. Jena's condition was worsening by the day. The number of anonymous letters reaching him had gone on increasing gradually. And the fact that every anonymous letter was yet another arrow of Shikhandi on the body of Dr. Jena – this was perhaps known very well to the unknown sender of the letters.

Bibhuprasad had long pondered over the place where these anonymous letters originated and who their sender was. What made the letters special was the fact that they did not arrive by post. Most of the time, they materialized on Dr. Jena's table by themselves. Of course, Dr. Jena's table was by the side of a window – and a letter could be slipped on to his table through a tiny opening in the window even when the window was firmly closed from the inside.

Observing the weakness of the window, Dr. Jena called a carpenter and sealed the window with a wooden board. But it was not as if the letters stopped coming after that. Even if they were not able to come to the table, they managed to get inside his room through the opening in the door. And they lay inside the room in such a state that they were discovered the moment the door was opened. And they were discovered in such a state that any self-conscious person would positively open them. Just as a suckling baby's terrified gaze learnt to discover the enlarged shadow of its tiny body far away from the light in the extreme darkness of the night however much one tried to hide it, and just as it enjoyed fulfilling the subconscious curiosity of its infancy by gazing lifelong at that darkness, so was every anonymous letter discovered by the person for whom it was meant. This is what made those letters special.

When Dr. Jena received the letter that day, he became extremely enraged for some reason. His anger arose because of his utter demoralisation and found its soft target in Bibhuprasad.

Of course, Bibhuprasad was equal to the task. If anyone had the necessary courage and patience to swim in the nectarous stream of ethical advice throughout his life, it was Bibhuprasad. The reason was that Bibhuprasad was the only creature among Natabar, Manmohan and Bibhuprasad who had made it a habit in his long life span to save himself by swimming simultaneously in the chilled waters of the Polar Regions as well as in the warm waters of the equatorial regions!

But it was a different kind of day.

It was the month of April. Clouds had started forming in the sky. Of course, they were simply collections of hot, visible gases. They contained no water in them. Layers of dust had gathered on the leaves of the deodar trees near the department. The delicate breaths of the spring were turning into the deep sighs of the storm. The green playground of the college had now turned into an arid desert. The summer had crept in sometime in the meanwhile.

Bibhuprasad was busy with his work. While examining the properties of matters extracted at some stage in his research on cassia oil, he was busy in making arrangements to convert them into materials to be used in the next stage of his research work.

When Dr. Jena had come to the laboratory that morning, he had cautioned Bibhuprasad, "Look! This is actually a complex phase of the research. When Dr. K., the eminent cancer researcher of America, was carrying on his work on a similar material, he had written that the material could be carcinogenic. So, take care! There is nothing to be afraid of; but be careful when you are working."

Bibhuprasad was busy with his work throughout that day. For some reason, he was in a happy mood. That harmonious, lonely moment in the laboratory without any competition had created some kind of an unknown possibility which had kept him engrossed for some reason in spite of all the uncertainties of research. Savouring that silent yet the most noiseful moment deep within him, Bibhuprasad was busy working with some breathless self-satisfaction.

For some reason, he had no complaints against life today. Neither Manmohan, nor Natabar – no one was able to get hold of him now – at this moment. He had only been looking at the creation around him, engrossed – his own creation! All those inert things of the laboratory – the artificial world of glasses and chemicals did not bother him like other days. On the other hand, his mind was filled with some kind of an inexplicable empathy looking at those bloated up, ugly and huge bottles.

"Yes! All these pregnant women …!"

"No, no – all these black, rustic creatures with enlarged spleen! Oh, dear …."

Bibhuprasad's mind was filled with some inexplicable inspiration for work. He was busy with his work.

There was the 'last light' outside – the phrase was normally used in military science. The time that a military general waited for – a commander about to attack!

The skin on Bibhuprasad's hand started to burn suddenly as he was busy with his work. He ran to the tap and washed his hand. Then he returned and started switching the lights on. At this time, his eyes fell on that light reflecting from the red bricks of the college building – the 'last light'.

The last light!

Bibhuprasad was startled. For some reason he was startled out of his wits.

Ordinarily, the natural colour reflecting from the college building looked terribly unnatural to his eyes! Terribly artificial! Terrible … terrible … really terrible!

Again, for some reason, someone seemed to remind him at that time about the warning of Dr. Jena –

"Look! This is indeed a complex phase. Dr. K., the American cancer researcher …."

But being a student of science there was no justifiable reason to be afraid of that warning of Dr. Jena. He was also not worried about that warning. What was there to be scared of? Was a student of medicine ever scared of the skeleton hanging in a corner of his laboratory? Was he ever afraid of the germs of cholera, leprosy, gonorrhea, diphtheria or tuberculosis kept under the lens of his microscope?

But, for some reason, Bibhuprasad could not carry the heavy burden of that terrible psychological moment any more and sat down. He was a research scholar in chemistry.

He started groaning suddenly – as if the extreme pressure of his brain was pressing him down – like a human head under the feet of a mammoth prehistoric elephant!

And its reason was like this –

Bibhuprasad entered his usual hotel that morning to have his lunch. An Indian chemistry student did not take a long time to finish his lunch. What took more time was to wash one's hands with soap and wait for the food to arrive with a virtuous mind – and quietly recite all those sweet verses and recall the wonderful fragrances relating to food! And, after that – when the saliva from around the tongue flowed to the full for that hungry moment – to disgorge all the pent up emotions on that half-dead man who came out with the food tray from the most stinking corner of the hotel.

But the situation that morning was even more complex. For some reason, rather than that man, the looks of his own soap-washed hand created a terrible reaction in his mind. He had already dipped his hand in the pot of dal in front of him by that time.

"Is this dal? This red and yellow water – you call it dal?"

Startled, Bibhuprasad pulled his hand out of the pot of dal – almost as if he had accidentally touched some poisonous chemical!

He wondered if it was not the colour produced by the hotel owner himself.

His mind was ill at ease. He called the manager of the Healthy Food Mart to him and wanted to know the truth. But the manager said emphatically, "Are you nuts? You haven't perhaps seen the turmeric powder of our hotel. We get it by the bagful from our regular source. Don't you cast blame upon the turmeric from Kandhamal! This is the limit! This is the limit!"

The manager spoke in a straightforward manner. The graveness of the voice convinced Bibhuprasad enough so that his hand automatically went inside his mouth.

However, another more important event occurred as he came out of the Healthy Food Mart. As he wiped his face after lunch and was busy in conversation with Basudev, the hotel owner, he noticed something else without really being aware of the implications. In his subconscious, Bibhuprasad had read the name of the chemical colour written on a small metal case kept on the manager's table.

However, the words 'Metanil Yellow' that was incongruous with other names like 'Bournvita', 'Horlicks', 'Ovaltine', 'Brooke Bond Tea', etc. to be found on the table had not bothered Bibhuprasad at the time.

Lost in the conversation with Basudev, Bibhuprasad had forgotten those two words at the time. Basudev had again reminded him, "The old man is losing the battle …. And do you know? Enemies are after him now. The headmaster of the school will retire very soon. But they won't allow the old man to become headmaster. They have applied to the Board. They have written lots of things against the old man. You sons are educated. Why don't you find someone who can help? Get acquainted with the officers who matter. Go! What do you gain by sitting only at home?"

Bibhuprasad had promised himself not to argue with such people. But it was difficult to hold back at times. But he laughed and said, "What do you people take me to be? You think my only work is to run to the officers at the drop of a feather? Someone comes from the village and says that some goons have taken away the standing crop. He advises me to run to the Police Sahib! Now you say that father cannot get the job that he wants and you too expect me to run to the concerned officers. What is this? Do you know that I am engaged in research here? Or do you think that I'm sitting here doing nothing?"

The last laugh of Basudev had subdued Bibhuprasad at that time for some reason.

Bibhuprasad had come away from the place wiping his face. And, after that – from ten in the morning till six in the evening, he had busied himself in that very significant phase of the research on cassia oil with rapt attention.

But – after that – when the 'last light' of the final part of the bright future of his research that was full of all kinds of possibilities fell in the eyes of Bibhuprasad! In that moment, Bibhuprasad was startled out of his wits like he had never been startled before! Only a researcher in chemistry could comprehend that the mention of the name of a chemical product could startle someone like that.

'Metanil yellow'? So, he had been eating this artificial chemical colour for the last five years? Had he slurped a few gallons of water containing the chemical assuming that it was dal? A few tonnes of poison would have gone inside his stomach along with an enormous quantity of food over the years!

By that time, 'metanil yellow', the artificial colour produced from coal tar, had started pouring the poison of Takshaka inside Bibhuprasad's head!

And, after that, everything that took place in the extrasensory kingdom of Bibhuprasad's poetic mind – all those were only the figments of his imagination. The more he examined the chemical properties of 'metanil yellow' in the obscure pages of his old text books, the more he felt that some psychologist was plucking out those obscure points of his memory and mind swiftly with his invisible needles.

When Bibhuprasad sat near the rectangular table

lying in a corner of the dark laboratory holding up that sunken cheek with a thin hand – he could perhaps visualize very well how he would be looking at someone observing him from a distance!

Yes, yes! He would be looking exactly like an old man – an old man, who has purchased all the materials needed for that definite, final day – wood, ghee, new clothes and all the other ancillary accompaniments! And, after that – he kept bargaining with those shopkeepers about the prices sitting amid the heap of materials – exactly like that … he must be looking exactly like that!

Bibhuprasad could recall all those scenes. He could clearly see – how he had been constantly drinking numerous other dangerous liquids like 'metanil yellow' – of different hues! He could see how, as a child, he was sipping several glasses of coloured water on the field where the Dola festival was held – sorbet! And he could also hear all those sounds – the shrieks coming from those coloured faces on that field, the breathless kirtans, the blaring concert of fighting scenes of the jatra and the captivating sound of the sirens fixed on the itinerant stalls which attracted people towards those coloured bottles.

Bibhuprasad stood for a while after wiping his hand over his head and stomach repeatedly; but he was not sure if he could digest those Atapis and Batapis inside his stomach.

Atapi and Batapi of that age!

And, what about those Atapis and Batapis that he had gone on creating over all these years!

The poisonous food stuff of years parked inside his stomach – who knew? And, in what other shapes Atapi and Batapi, those demons of the Puranic age, have been after these simple, innocent and gullible Indians!

Bibhuprasad recalled – the warnings that he had heard from a well-meaning, elderly person sitting across from him in the hotel as he was about to take a piece of roti. The man had warned him that day in the same voice that Dr. Jena had used to caution him this morning. He asked, "Are you eating rotis?"

Bibhuprasad initially thought that the man was an idiot. Hence, he too had tried to answer the idiotic question of the man in the same half-witted manner.

But the man had ignored the sarcasm of Bibhuprasad and tried to explain things as if he was his own son.

"Listen, son! It's all right that you are taking rotis. But be a little careful."

"Careful?" The roti in Bibhuprasad's hand had stopped midway. Looking at the man's face, he had put it back on the plate.

Picking up a newspaper lying near him, the man pointed at a news item – the government notification for people eating rotis.

Bibhuprasad's lower jaw gradually drooped down in fear. And saliva was dripping from the mouth – the drops of saliva meant for the roti that had come near the mouth and returned to the plate – on the pages of the newspaper.

"Were you not aware of this?" the man asked again.

Bibhuprasad remained quiet looking at the kind lips of the elderly man.

"Don't eat roti ever again. Remember this advice of mine, son! Flour and oil – stay away from these two things in this age. Don't you see this with your own eyes? What you were about to eat just now – these rotis! Who knows? Who can say that these have not been made from the bag of flour mentioned in that government notification? Many people say that this flour has been imported from abroad.

And some rat poison has accidentally got mixed with these as they were being brought in a ship.

"The nine hundred people who died recently in a volunteers' training camp in Kerala – apparently, they died after eating rotis made from such flour! Oh, God!"

Night had fallen. The last light of the sun on the red brick walls of the college had died down since long. And in its place, there was darkness. Bibhuprasad switched on the lights of the laboratory.

He could think of nothing else after that. He stood up – as he collected the papers and notes relating to his research lying scattered on the table, he stumbled suddenly. His elbow hit a corner of the table. Bibhuprasad groaned in pain for a moment. He sat down again.

Bibhuprasad was slightly apprehensive to discover an envelope from the pile of papers lying on his table even as every nerve centre in his body was throbbing with pain.

As he pulled out the envelope amid that pain and apprehension, tore it open and looked at the letter, he discovered the sender's name to be as irksome as the name of the sender of an anonymous letter.

'Radha' – that mocking name at the end of the letter seemed to slap Bibhuprasad hard across his ear.

Bibhuprasad's head spun like a top.

Something took hold of him after that. A dreaded devil seemed to descend down from space on to Bibhuprasad's shoulders. Bibhuprasad ran straightaway to the door of Dr. Jena with the letter in hand and threw it inside that lonely, dark room like the remnant of the ground ball of iron inside the stomach of Shamba.

And, after that – he turned back.

ELEVEN

Bibhuprasad turned back – the way he had never turned back earlier in his life!

He had no other thought when he locked the laboratory that evening. His only thought was how he would return to his house and make a hearth on one side of the tiny verandah – a small hearth of the most primary type consisting of three bricks. He would turn his attention to other things only after doing that. Then he would go to the market to buy the various things needed for cooking – a pile of wood, a small pot, a ladle, a small cauldron, and perhaps, a sauce pan. Then he would buy rice, dal and vegetables for at least today. He would leave for the village in the morning and carry back provisions for at least one month from there. He would be able to continue with his research only then. He could not eat in the hotel even a day longer and knowingly ruined his valuable life in the process – through poisonous food, inedible food or lack of food.

He had already prepared a routine for himself in his mind. When he would get up, when he would cook and come to the laboratory; but he had not been able to decide upon one thing until then – and it was Natabar.

Natabar had started bothering Bibhuprasad like the proverbial camel inside the tent as the days progressed. It was not possible to drive him out of the house nor was it possible to keep him there. Matters had been somehow under control till now; but who knew what might happen once the cooking started in the house! Would he cooperate with Bibhuprasad in cooking? Even if he did – would he involve himself in cooking or insist on engaging a cook? It would be difficult to find anyone immediately. Even if a cook was available, he would demand a hefty salary. Of course, there was no question of engaging a cook these days. Who would guard him? And if there was no one at home to keep a watch over the cook, that home was worse than any hotel.

Bibhuprasad had been walking thus thinking about the pros and con of cooking – towards his house. He was walking just like a disciple of the Vedic age. And he was the kind of disciple who had come to gather knowledge – not from his father or in the ashram of the gurus – but from Yama himself.

Bibhuprasad was walking today with a strong determination to erect the hearth in his house. He was walking – leaving behind his beloved cassia oil laboratory – he was walking fast today with firm steps. He did not feel sentimental in the least looking at the surroundings – the flower plant behind him, the multi-coloured windows of the laboratory, the sun dial, the marble plaque near the portico, the Muchukunda plant or the rows of deodar trees in front. He neither looked at nor recalled those danger signals of the days gone by.

"What I was saying, brother! Science? If you want him to fail, admit him into I.Sc. Was I not telling you?"

Or –

"Take Arts, son! Take Arts! Art is life! Science is transient ...." Bibhuprasad was walking with a mission. There was only one objective for him now – the hearth! That's all!

But that determined walk of his was somewhat hindered as he reached the College Square. He met Abu Mian – his school mate. Abu Mian was returning from the village. It was not possible to avoid him as he had met him suddenly after a long time. Apart from that, Abu Mian was also quite a spectacle! That gait of his! He looked like a trader of valuable gems from the Arabian Nights! Who would not be stupefied upon seeing his bicycle and the clusters of pearl or diamond hanging from each of the bundles! Abu Mian brought eggs from the villages and sold them in the town.

Abu Mian was very happy to see Bibhuprasad. Bringing his bicycle to a stop very carefully and standing by its side, Abu Mian smiled with the airs of a successful man in life and said, "So, brother! Where are you now?"

Examining those clusters of pearls hanging from all sides of Abu Mian with the greedy looks of a grape-hungry jackal, Bibhuprasad only pointed at the red building behind him – the college building.

The carefree smile of Abu Mian was not in the least diminished; rather, it broadened even more. Very happily, he again asked, "Oh! Professor Sahib! You've become a professor now, no?"

Bibhuprasad leaned towards Abu Mian's cycle. He answered Abu Mian's question caressing the baskets of eggs with the fingers of a spectator in a museum.

No one knew what Abu Mian made of that answer of Bibhuprasad, but he stopped in his tracks and said with his mouth gaping, "Hey! You've become such a big man in these last few years? You've become a research scholar!"

Mustering enough courage, Bibhuprasad pushed his hand inside Abu Mian's basket to pick up two large farm eggs, and as he felt its Koh-I-Noor like warmth with his cheeks, lips and chin, he asked, "Brother! Do you have any objection if I want to buy a couple of these?"

For some reason, Abu Mian, the businessman, suddenly felt gratified. Handing over two more eggs to Bibhuprasad, he said, "Brother! What're you saying? Take them. Take a few more! This is nothing! What could I give to such a big man like you? You're a research scholar, no …?"

Only God knew why Abu Mian was beholden to those two words – research scholar. Perhaps, he associated the word 'scholar' with some prestigious word like 'scholarship'. Bibhuprasad recalled how he was scared of these 'scholars' in his own school days. Those who got scholarship from the minor school were extremely competitive at their studies. Abu Mian was also one of them. He had got scholarship in the minor school. Of course, he had got the scholarship in the category reserved for Muslims. But no one knew what happened to him after that. Abu Mian had simply vanished from the school in the tenth class. And this was the same Abu Mian who Bibhuprasad was envying today.

Bibhuprasad talked with Abu Mian for a long time after that. Finally, Abu Mian again smiled expansively with the airs of a successful businessman as he said, "Brother! Just supply the eggs! I take the responsibility of dealing with the public. And do you know something? I've just taken up something even bigger. I've now become a wholesale dealer in eggs. My target is to send at least a wagon of eggs everyday to Calcutta. I would really appreciate it if you helped me in this work. There is a great future in Orissa now for poultry farming. This is the time to join the bandwagon. You're a scientist – you would simply love this work. This is independent work. If it clicks, you would be rich beyond imagination in a year or two! You've no idea how the market for eggs is picking up day by day. Take the trouble of dropping in at my Buxi Bazar godown – you would see for yourself! How much vitamin comes out of eggs and how much vitamin is there in this business – you just need one glance at my godown to know things for yourself!"

Pocketing the four valuable eggs from the basket of Abu Mian, Bibhuprasad again caressed his pearl-laden bicycle. When Abu Mian left, he again proceeded towards his house – that is, towards the hearth.

But the accidental meeting with Abu Mian, his practical advice, and, above all, the scene of his royal, aesthetic get-up of the Baghdadi, stinking rich trader had so influenced Bibhuprasad that he thought that someone was pulling him by the hand to lead him to some Garden of Eden on earth – where, he was able to see those wonderful scenes standing in the last scene of 'The Divine Comedy'.

When Bibhuprasad was feeling the life-giving touch of those basic matters over and over again by repeatedly touching the four eggs inside his pockets with the tip of his extremely sensitive fingers, his hereditary, geographic mind could easily imagine at the time all social, economic, political, scientific, and, above all, those universal poetic angles related to that.

He remembered – how, imagining the scene of rearing of sheep in the Downs grazing ground of Australia while studying geography, he had told his father, "Father! Why don't we rear sheep? Let us keep a herd of sheep and become rich by exporting wool and meat worldwide."

TWELVE

Cooking had started without any hitch at Bibhuprasad's place. What was more important, Natabar too had joined Bibhuprasad in cooking. Realizing the unwholesomeness and hazardous nature of the food available in the hotels, both of them had thrown themselves headlong into cooking in the 'Niraba Nilaya' mess of Bibhuprasad. But the plan to start the chemical cottage industry of Natabar suddenly ran into trouble. A letter arrived for him that day from the village, "Come immediately if you want to see your mother alive. Don't forget to carry some fruits with you …."

Natabar sat brooding as he turned the letter over a few times. Bibhuprasad had no idea until then about the contents of the letter.

After returning from the laboratory that day, Bibhuprasad too was helping Natabar in collecting old torch light batteries as also those 'cat with nine lives' mark batteries used in radios for his proposed ferrous ammonium sulphate industry. Apart from preparing a list of the friends in the city in possession of battery-operated radios, another wonderful idea had struck Bibhuprasad

Bibhuprasad said to Natabar, "Look! All rich men and institutions start from the beginning – that is, starting from the scratch. Besides, when a scientist wants to remedy a situation, he looks to the basic origin of the problem. Our problem now is hunger and poverty. If we want to solve these problems, we have to start again from the beginning.

Of course, you are my forerunner in thinking about such things. Hence, I've decided to help you in the work relating to the chemical cottage industry. But think about it once. This chemical cottage industry of yours is not the basic remedy. We have to first fight against hunger. Hence, we've to start really from the beginning – and that is cultivation."

Natabar had not been able to understand the real meaning of what Bibhuprasad wanted to say. He ridiculed him to say, "All right. Let me discover a new process of cultivation in the atmosphere; you would start after that."

However, Bibhuprasad had not lost heart. He wanted to demonstrate how his dream would work. He said, "Look! You've a completely wrong idea about things. You think one cannot start farming unless he has fifty to sixty acres of land. But you see! I've already written to my father – he's going to retire soon – he'd get a lump sum towards his provident fund and pension. I'd start with that money and the five acres of land that we have in the village. Let's see what happens. It would be an experiment! The land is quite fertile; it's by the side of the canal. By the grace of Ravenshaw Sahib, we've not only been educated in his college – the Taladanda Canal flows near our village like the writings of his pen! You haven't seen that land, Natabar! I think – if someone sincerely starts even with those five acres – only cauliflowers and tomatoes! Ah! He would be stinking rich in five years. Why? If a cauliflower sells for one rupee, five thousand cauliflowers would fetch five thousand rupees! And how much land is needed for a crop of five thousand cauliflowers!"

The work of the chemical cottage industry of Natabar and Bibhuprasad had continued amid these flights of fancy. And, in competition with Natabar, Bibhuprasad was also planning to start a small poultry farm on an experimental basis – within the small confines of 'Niraba Nilaya'. He had not yet consumed those four eggs given by Abu Mian. He was getting ready to prove his firm determination about farming before Natabar. He said for the benefit of Natabar, "Okay, look! Look at these four eggs. See what I am able to do with these four eggs as my capital before I leave for the village."

As Bibhuprasad was busy creating a thermostat by keeping a biscuit tin over a lantern and using a laboratory thermometer to hatch the eggs, that obstructive letter arrived from Natabar's village.

Bibhuprasad was at a loss to understand why Natabar seemed suddenly lost to the world even as they were proceeding smoothly in their work. He asked Natabar in jest, "What happened? Has the Blue Lily been written again? I'm telling you – go and get her here. It won't be enough to be economical only about food these days. One also has to be economical in matrimonial affairs. Go and bring your Blue Lily here – it's getting increasingly difficult to manage this place without a female around."

The Blue Lily about whom Bibhuprasad was teasing Natabar at the time was the same Blue Lily about whom Natabar used to talk quite often – about whom Natabar talked while smelling the heaps of bird manure near the college gate and talking about the love letter of his Calcutta-returned uncle and his memsahib. The girl who had inserted a letter inside the trouser pocket of Natabar in the waking hours of all those ghouls and witches just before the dawn broke on the day of Khudurukuni Osha – this was the same Blue Lily – the basic Blue Lily – whose fragrance Bibhuprasad had associated with Murasha in due course.

However, Natabar seemed to be the least interested in Bibhuprasad's banter. On the other hand, he roared like a cobra suddenly and said, "Give me a *lathi,* brother! I'll first kill that government postmaster. Only then I'll go to the village – for the *shraadh* ceremony of my mother."

Bibhuprasad was taken aback by this sudden explosion of Natabar and he was so startled that he was not aware when he had put the weight of his hand on an egg.

Natabar was fuming by that time. He shouted, "Look! I'm not my father's son if I don't smash the head of that government postmaster today! And, if I find mother dead when I reach the village, I'll implicate that man in a murder case. He has killed. He has killed my mother definitely! It's his government! The government of that postmaster has killed my mother today, friend … it has killed."

Bibhuprasad did all he could to pacify him and got hold of the letter with a great deal of difficulty. Then he understood everything. He saw the postage mark on the letter and understood why Natabar had exploded the way he did. He had no further doubt that Natabar had enough justification to get infuriated. Of course, there was no time to find the reason why a letter took ten days to reach a distance of forty miles.

Bibhuprasad tried to put Natabar in a proper frame of mind and said, "Look! This is not the time to run to court to file a suit against the postal department in stead of finding out the state of your mother. It is our duty to first take care of the basic things. Go to the village as quickly as possible – make sure that she's all right!"

"But why did that rogue hold up my letter? Who's responsible for this?" Natabar still shouted at the top of his voice.

Anyway, Bibhuprasad helped Natabar to gain his composure once again. He made him understand that the postal department was actually not to be blamed for the lapse. Natabar's own people were at fault. The first mistake was to send an ordinary letter in an emergency like this. It's no use blaming the well-meaning person who has committed this mistake; at least, he has been kind enough to write the letter. Apart from that, it was fortunate that the letter reached Natabar at all from his remote village where people within a radius of ten miles might never have seen a post office. Hence, Natabar did not have a right to say anything except to curse his fate – there was no point in blaming the poor postmaster of the city for the lapse.

Bibhuprasad then accompanied Natabar to the postmaster of the same post office. He withdrew fifty rupees from his pass book and Natabar left for the village. Of course, Bibhuprasad had received six hundred rupees in the meantime towards the arrears of research scholarship for the last six months. Before leaving for the village, Bibhuprasad cautioned him, "Look! Bring some fruits with you. And be careful! Don't quarrel with the fruit stall owners again. They know you. And the swelling on your forehead is still there to identify you. Don't quarrel with those people. Just accept whatever they give you. And, if you find the old lady to be really ill, bring her back to Cuttack immediately with you."

Dispatching Natabar to his village, Bibhuprasad again returned to the post office. He bought a post card and wrote a letter to his father, "Father! I heard from Basudev, the owner of the Healthy Food Mart, that you are retiring from service. In fact, I'm happy to get this news. I'm happy that you are being released from the slavery of your service life.

"Yes, my life as a research scholar has come to an end because of vitiating circumstances. The situation in our department is terrible. Manmohan, about whom

I had talked to you some time back, has returned again. My research guide Dr. Jena has his own problems. We've heard that he is getting ready to leave research and join the Bhoodan Movement of Vinoba Bhave. In the circumstances, I don't have any other option except to go back to the village.

"But there is no reason to worry. I'm not bothered in the least. On the other hand, I feel a great deal encouraged to hear that you're retiring. You should immediately apply for your provident fund deposits and pension. I've made certain plans. If I don't turn out to be a world famous agriculturist in five years ...."

For some reason, Bibhuprasad stopped short near the letter box after posting the letter. He inserted his hand through the opening in the letter box and groped around. Then he thought better of it and decided that it would not be proper to get the letter back from the box. Then he returned to his house and got busy with the production of the thermostat to hatch the eggs.

Only then, Bibhuprasad discovered the accident that had taken place in the morning. The egg that had cracked under the weight of his hand – Bibhuprasad was startled to see the tiny eyes, beak and legs of the chick and the red ants surrounding the shell. He was startled the same way as he had been one day in his childhood – the day he had killed that golden oriole chick with a catapult – during a summer vacation a long time ago – the day his mother lay in bed due to illness – and a tiny, black bird flew around their house for months on end – a bird that was considered to be ill-omened – Bibhuprasad had been infuriated with the bird and killed that golden oriole chick by mistake.

Bibhuprasad shivered for some reason. He told himself – looking at that ball of meat surrounded by ants, "Oh, no! Its mother had perhaps been warming it when

Abu Mian's agent might have snatched it from under her belly."

Bibhuprasad recalled again – that marathon running that day. He picked up that golden oriole chick lying on the ground with a broken neck and blew in its ear and nose.

A few red ants had been swarming on their feathers by the time. He ran first to the image of Gramadevati nearby. Gramadevati – who sat inside a hollow in a banyan tree at the edge of the village with her red head sticking out – who stared unceasingly at the outside world with her frightening eyes – at the entire village, the entire country and the entire universe! Who sat in judgment over all the sins and virtues of the world! And who reviewed the deeds of an ignorant human child when he begged her forgiveness!

Supplicating fervently for the dead chick, the child Bibhuprasad prayed, "Mother! I'll sacrifice this finger before you like Ekalavya if you bring this chick back to life!"

Smearing the chick all over with the vermillion of the goddess, Bibhuprasad waited for hours.

Then he got up and ran again. He ran to the temple of Shiva. Not getting any help there, he turned back again. He remembered suddenly then – their family priest once said that there was a book of scriptures in their puja room which contained a mantra – which was known as the Mahamrityunjay Mantra and a dead person could be brought alive by reciting it.

As he turned breathless amid all these running around – Bibhuprasad could recall – the way he had surrendered to his father.

"Father! Father! There is no deliverance for me any more, father! I've committed a grave sin, father!' the child Bibhuprasad broke into sobs.

And he remembered too how his father had consoled

him that day. Picking up the child in his lap, father had whispered in his ears – his ailing mother was groaning in pain in the adjacent room – and Bhabaniprasad had been consoling the son, "Son! Do you know who this dead chick really is? This is Compassion! Seeing the death of one such bird, Maharshi Valmiki had written the Ramayana. You've turned into a great poet if the death of this chick has filled you with the same nectar-like compassion. In order to bring this dead chick back to life, why are you running hither and thither in stead of writing a Ramayana for it? And, if someone cannot write a Ramayana, how can he make use of the Mahamrityunjay Mantra? How can his holy pot of water have the power to bring someone back to life …?"

The death of the golden oriole chick, the woeful scene of the dead embryo of Abu Mian's egg, poisonous food stuff, the highhandedness of Natabar and so on – Bibhuprasad tried to forget all these and concentrated on his new project of manufacturing the thermostat machine with the help of his hurricane lantern, biscuit tin and the thermometer.

X X X X X

Bibhuprasad heard that his research guide Prof. Jena was ill and bed-ridden for the past seven days when he went that day to the laboratory. No one knew what he was suffering from. He didn't allow anyone to come near him. He didn't talk to anyone. He didn't permit anyone to meet him except a saffron-clad monk who had materialized strangely from some place.

That day Bibhuprasad heard a strange rumour when he went to the tea club. Harish told him about the illness of Prof. Jena. Harish whispered in Bibhuprasad's ears, "Sir, it's as good as a detective novel! Someone wrote an anonymous letter to him. What rascals are there in this world! As such, the old man gets scared easily. But another anonymous letter came to the old man! The sender had written that she would commit suicide if the old man didn't meet her on a specified date at a specified place. The old man shook like a leaf when he got that letter. Could you blame him for that? It's not that – but have you heard that rumour that is making the rounds?"

Bibhuprasad shivered looking at the expression on the old man's face.

Harish, however, had not noticed the change of expression on Bibhuprasad's face. He bent further towards Bibhuprasad and whispered that one sentence. Then he slithered away from the place.

Bibhuprasad stood up. He felt as if the ground was slipping from beneath his feet.

At this time, a few elderly lecturers entered the tea club. They had a pencil and a long sheet of paper to make arithmetical calculations. They sat down around that sheet of paper.

Bibhuprasad had no idea why they were shouting so loudly at the time. But he knew that the revised report of the Pay Commission had been released at that time and that report had kept the intellectuals of the country engaged in complex mathematics.

And, just at that time, a research scholar called Bibhuprasad was running on the streets of the city. His research guide was almost mad. There was no trace of his friend Natabar. His father was about to retire. And, what hurt most was that rumour – where his poetry had committed suicide! When Bibhuprasad got no trace of Murasha after looking for her everywhere in the city, he was convinced that the rumour that was making the rounds about Murasha was true. The rustic and grave voice of old man Harish hit his ears time and again. It was as if he was repeatedly saying, "Sir! The sister of that widowed nurse – that dame studying at the college – has she really committed suicide? And do you know? The girl was eight months gone. Manmohan Babu had promised to marry her; but we hear that she's already dead! Manmohan Babu refused to marry her! Oh, God! What has come over this earth!"

THIRTEEN

Bibhuprasad returned to his house that day immersed in all kinds of thoughts, misgivings, apprehensions and doubts. He reached the house with a preoccupied mind. As usual, he shoved his hand inside the pocket to get the key to the front door. He suddenly found the door to be unlocked at the time. The door was closed from the inside.

Bibhuprasad was amazed.

Had Natabar returned?

Bibhuprasad knocked on the door. But there was no response from inside.

The day was coming to an end. Outside, there was the last light of that 'metanil yellow' evening. The earth had a weary look around it. Only the old parrot shouted from the verandah of the contractor's house – "Radha! Radha!"

But Bibhuprasad had no ears for that today. Like the motor horn of the contractor or the siren of the hume pipe factory every morning and evening, the speciality of the bird's calls had been lost on Bibhuprasad that evening.

Bibhuprasad's anxiety increased manifold when there was no response from inside in spite of his repeated knockings on the door.

For some reason, he concluded that Natabar had returned from the village and had done something inconceivable out of grief because his mother had expired.

He was scared now – did that fellow find this one

place in the whole wide world to commit suicide? Here? In Bibhuprasad's house?

Physical exhaustion and mental distress were gradually taking their toll on Bibhuprasad. His weak knees ached terribly having roamed here and there throughout the day.

Unable to contain himself any longer, he shrieked, "Rascal! This fellow has ruined me!" Then he lifted a foot and kicked viciously at the door.

The door was flung open. The image of a woman caught unawares revealed itself from within.

Bibhuprasad stopped in his tracks.

He saw a woman – slightly dark, medium height and in strange clothes – a strange woman wearing a strange gown, something akin to a Japanese kimono – she had been suddenly discovered as she was trying to get out of her strange attire and get into her familiar artificial silk sari.

Bibhuprasad was startled. He was as startled as the prince in the fairy tale the day he might have discovered the Brahmin frog transforming into a woman – who might have been suddenly discovered by the prince while roaming around as a beautiful woman after coming out very discreetly from the covering of the frog.

Bibhuprasad stared at her for a long moment. It was such a long moment that his blazing eyes had turned a lot softer and two drops of liquid wax had dropped down from the tearful eyes of the image that had become one with the wall on the opposite side – in the shape of two long, exclamatory marks!

Bibhuprasad drew in a long breath and retraced a few steps from inside the room. The familiar, romantic fragrance of a blue lily hit his nose suddenly at that time – and he recalled an afternoon long past – the day Murasha had been discovered for the first time – those books slipping out of her hands – the flower ….

Of course, the woman had recovered enough by that time. She came out of the wall now and faced Bibhuprasad with quiet confidence. There was no veil on her head and that frightened look was no longer there in her eyes. However, the drop of tear in the corner of her eye had not dried yet.

Bibhuprasad took stock of things inside his 'Niraba Nilaya' in one glance. The dirty shirt of Natabar was hanging from a nail on the wall – the one he had worn while leaving for the village. There was a large bundle of clothes lying in one corner of the room. A strangely dented trunk … and what was that … may be a mridangam covered with a red cloth, and a wooden box … it was perhaps a box holding a harmonium.

Bibhuprasad was amazed. He wondered what it was all about. Had Natabar come with a jatra party?

Bibhuprasad continued to stand outside. His feet ached terribly. But he could not get inside his house.

Suddenly, he had all kinds of misgivings. He wondered if Natabar was not taking a page out of the advocate's book and plotting to throw him out of his own house.

He was scared. He thought – Natabar could drink alcohol, play on the flute in the middle of the night and make all kinds of noises to frighten the enceinte wife of the advocate; but what could he do? How would he throw these camels-in-tent outside?

Bibhuprasad was really worried now. Where would he go now? This was his house – the only shelter he had. His clothes, bed, books and other belongings were there.

Bibhuprasad looked inside the room again with

baleful eyes. The Sambalpuri bed sheet had been spread across his bed neatly. But ….

Finally, Bibhuprasad stood up in sheer desperation. All that litter – scrap iron, tin plates, torchlight batteries, all those signboards – he stood up to get away from all those stinking things.

Bibhuprasad was startled to hear a wonderful voice exactly at that time.

The woman was rushing towards the hearth at that time tying the corner of her sari around her waist – to that hearth, of course – one that Bibhuprasad had made with his own hands a few days back.

She struck something with a flourish of her hand to light the fire in the hearth. Bibhuprasad observed the first flash of light – it was a light of a different kind – it could not have been the ordinary light of a matchstick – it was the light of a cigarette lighter.

"Let the curse of high heavens come upon me!" she started the chirping of a golden oriole chick in that sweet voice of hers, "Nata Bhai had told me time and again – to serve snacks and tea when his friend arrived – how could I forget it so quickly!"

Bibhuprasad's thinking faculty had stopped working by then. He was only having a strong and basic experience with fear, amazement and surrounding mystery. They all seemed to be fairy tales – for Bibhuprasad.

He was observing only one thing then – how two extraordinary hands were creating the holy fire inside that confined space resembling a small pit of holy fire – a family fire!

Bibhuprasad was amazed – when he remembered about all those strange people – those who would have started that fire for the first time – those who would have created that basic fire in the fireless caves of mountains leaving their homes and princely pleasures behind to live in the forests in order to ensure that the promises made by their fathers or brothers were not violated – which they would have consecrated with their basic chanting and by which they themselves would have been consecrated – along with their hunger!

It was not yet completely dark. The blaze of the fire from the hearth was not so evident in the background of the last light of the sun. The newly arrived woman was quite busy in her work at the time. Bibhuprasad had been enveloped by a beautiful fragrance of light snacks by that time.

In a moment, the woman placed a plate of halwa on a strange-looking china plate and a cup of tea before Bibhuprasad and stood to a side.

A long, silent moment passed after that. Bibhuprasad could not understand what he should do in that impossible moment. He was about to say something when an unnatural event took place again.

"Damn me! I forgot! As he left for the hospital, Nata Bhai had told me to ask you before serving food – whether you would eat the food prepared by me – we are sweepers by caste …."

"Sweepers?" Bibhuprasad was startled. So, this was not the blue lily? To say the truth, Bibhuprasad's head reeled for a moment looking at that china plate. The genteelness of the strange gown, cigarette lighter, china plate, mridangam and harmonium – which had embraced Bibhuprasad's mind like the arms of a giant octopus a while ago – they were falling down – receding away – coming unstuck, in a way.

Bibhuprasad stopped short – he stopped like the

hand of a high-ranking officer drawing a thousand rupees a month as his salary – the hand which stopped over the plate of food served for him when he discovered a subordinate employee drawing a salary of thirty rupees a month eating beside him.

But, in a moment, the woman changed her voice totally. Bibhuprasad was startled. He hadn't yet forgotten the frog-turned-woman of the fairy tales.

Without giving any time to Bibhuprasad to think any further about her, the woman again threw a bait of genteelness towards Bibhuprasad, and the next moment, she legitimized her personality like a psychologist in the mind of a highly educated person like Bibhuprasad.

"But – I don't know whether Nata Bhai would have told you or not – my father works in a Japanese ship called Honshu …."

Bibhuprasad could piece everything together now. That strange chintz dress was really a Japanese dress – that was called a kimono – the picture of which he had seen in his Class II text book for the first time – the live picture of that hospitable Japanese girl suddenly emerged with bubbles from under the depthless muddy sea of Bibhuprasad's mind – she unfolded her live blue petals slowly again and bloomed at the highest level of the mud in his mind.

"Blue Lily?" Bibhuprasad was really startled and stared straight at that face now.

Blue Lily! Bibhuprasad again pronounced silently.

Bibhuprasad no longer heard the voice of the woman. His hand had started moving from the plate to the mouth and from the mouth to the plate.

Masticating the cardamom seeds, Bibhuprasad was looking around him sitting on the veranda of his small, tin-roofed house. Only he knew what he was thinking, staring openmouthed at the boundary walls of the increasing number of two-storied and three-storied houses, the huge godowns of paddy and potato, and the hume pipe factory!

He finished the cup of tea with one gulp after that and got up; but something made him turn around and look inside the house.

It was as if a new responsibility had come upon him. Putting something inside a small aluminium can, the woman put it before Bibhuprasad and ordered him in a wonderful, familiar manner, "Nata Bhai had said – you would have to carry the barley to the hospital for my mother."

"Hospital?" In a strange way, Bibhuprasad's voice had become very clear by then. There was no hesitancy in it.

"Has Natabar brought his mother along with him? How's she?" Only then Bibhuprasad recalled Natabar's situation.

The woman started weeping suddenly.

There was no further doubt in Bibhuprasad's mind. He was sure that Natabar's mother had expired in the meanwhile. Bibhuprasad was not in the least bothered by the weeping of the woman. On the other hand, he was feeling good – the idea that a woman would ever start weeping in his 'Niraba Nilaya' seemed so queer to him. Rather, he recalled that wicked Gurkha at the time who once lived under that tin roof.

Not wishing to interrupt the woman in her weeping, Bibhuprasad picked up that barley can; but he turned back after walking a few paces to ask, "Which ward in the hospital? Has Natabar said anything?"

As she blew on the glass of a hurricane lantern and wiped it, the woman answered, "Nata Bhai hasn't told me anything – he had only asked me to make snacks for you and to ask you to carry the barley to the hospital if he was late."

"All right. Do you know what she is suffering from? I could make further enquiries if I knew that."

"I've no idea. But Nata Bhai was worried. He reached the village six days after the death of his mother. The rituals were finished only yesterday and he brought us here this morning. But he was saying that the disease was not very serious. It would be cured easily with a bit of surgery."

Bibhuprasad turned and walked at a fast pace towards the surgical ward of the hospital.

FOURTEEN

Bibhuprasad discovered Natabar on the street that day. Natabar and a rustic woman sitting near him – an elderly woman – they were returning in a rickshaw. Bibhuprasad could recognize Natabar the moment he saw his shaven head and confused face and stopped the rickshaw.

But Bibhuprasad was suddenly startled to see that dolorous face of Natabar and the strange smile on his lips that was totally incongruous with that face. Natabar's face looked quite frightening at the time. He looked like the messenger of death of Tolstoy's story – who had been cursed to come to the earth as he had once succumbed to a strange human weakness, and for expressing an inexcusable doubt about the laws of God – in the shape of a human being – in order to understand the harsh truth of the Creation from man – what men live by?

"I was going to you with the barley … what's wrong with this old woman? Why, she does not look very ill!" In order to avoid that mysterious gaze of Natabar, Bibhuprasad stared at the woman sitting on the rickshaw a bit more minutely.

The woman looked exactly like that – simple and uncomplicated like her daughter; but she looked even sweeter. It was perhaps the compassion on her face – a sanguine, ever ready compassion! Her rustic clothes, the veil on her head, the *paan* in her mouth, an indication of her expectant manner and limitless patience mixed with her frightened glances and the depth of her eyes held the gaze of Bibhuprasad in a way that was clearly distinct from the mysterious looks on Natabar's face.

"This is Sukumari's mother ...." Natabar finally answered Bibhuprasad's question; but he suddenly fell quiet after that. As if he was irritated upon seeing Bibhuprasad with the can of barley.

But Natabar was not actually angry with anyone at the time. He was only amazed and going over that question repeatedly in his mind – hadn't he been cursed and sent to the earth to find the answer to that question? That one question – 'What men live by?"

The two friends returned to 'Niraba Nilaya' that evening one after the other. The rickshaw carrying Sukumari's mother was in the front. The elderly woman looked back at intervals to run her compassionate eyes on the two men following her. Natabar's gaze was fixed on the image of the woman. He was still smiling that strange smile – silently.

The old woman's rickshaw finally stopped in front of 'Niraba Nilaya' – and Natabar suddenly whispered in Bibhuprasad's ears with a deep sigh, "This is not goiter or some such thing, Bibhuprasad – this is malignant tumour!" Natabar continued in the hurtful voice of the 'camel hair cap' days of yore, "Cancer has taken hold of her now – breast cancer!"

"Cancer? So, you have brought a cancer patient with you now?" Bibhuprasad seemed to have a start, "Is she going to stay with us now?" Bibhuprasad suddenly thought about that advocate and his family.

But there was something else that evening apart from the regrets, fear, sorrow and helplessness that had attracted Bibhuprasad deeply towards them. Bibhuprasad had assimilated even more with them – those unknown 'camels-in-tent' people.

They wanted Bibhuprasad as their special guest that evening.

It didn't take long for Bibhuprasad to get acquainted with the old woman. The way a rustic woman, especially from a poor, uneducated, Harijan family, considered herself to be a lesser being and maintained her distance from the more privileged people, and pushed herself to the lowest strata of the society of her own volition – such things could not be seen from the conduct of that strange family. Hence, Bibhuprasad didn't find it too difficult to mingle with them. Besides, Natabar stood firmly between them, i.e. between Bibhuprasad and the two women – as their interpreter.

"You'll have dinner with us tonight," Natabar was the first to invite Bibhuprasad.

Sukumari's mother came next. She had changed in the meantime. She had even gone to the municipality tap in front of the house and had a wash. Three bricks had been arranged in a corner of the verandah laced with mud to make a hearth. Sukumari was busy with her work by that time. A breeze was blowing across the hearth. The flame of the fire was flying from one side to the other under the small pot.

Bibhuprasad was bewildered. What were they burning? Wherefrom did they collect firewood?

But they knew – just as an ant knew the way to its hole, they knew their way around. Bibhuprasad saw – lots of dry sticks, hay, grass, wild bush, etc. near the hearth – gathered from inside the compound of the house where Bibhuprasad was planning to start his poultry farm. There was no dearth of firewood for Sukumari – inside the tiny compound. Hence, making a fire inside the hearth was not a problem for her – for the two industrious hands of hers.

The old woman came and sat near her daughter – to help her out.

"No, no, mother! Don't come here. Don't sit near the fire. You'll get worse." Sukumari didn't allow her mother to do anything.

"Come on! What's wrong with me? This boy has needlessly brought me to Cuttack. Why? Nothing is wrong with me! I just have a bit of backache and I had a fever a few days back. I tried to dissuade him – what was the necessity of bringing me to Cuttack? Such a costly place – oh, dear! I'll leave for the village tomorrow morning. I don't need this city! One *paan* costs four paise here! I had never seen anything like this!"

"Mother, what did the doctor say after examining you?" Sukumari was grinding spices sitting a few feet away. She had discovered a smooth piece of stone in the meantime to grind the spices.

"Hey! Haven't you put cardamom in the spices? There is absolutely no fragrance! Oh dear, oh, dear! What kind of curry are you going to cook? That other son is going to eat with us – don't you know? Have we called him so lovingly just to serve any trash? Didn't I tell you while going for my bath to open that box and get the packet of spices inside it? There's cardamom, cloves, cinnamon, cubebs, nutmegs … hadn't your father brought all these? That time when he had brought that chintz dress for you from Japan … that kimono or something …."

The two friends had sat on a charpoy a few feet away – Natabar and Bibhuprasad. It was quite dark by that time. The hurricane lantern had been burning – the bright light inside that polished glass at evening time. Besides, there was the fire of the hearth there. The beautiful, homely fragrance of dal being cooked moved in the air mixed with the smoke. The wonderful fragrance of the spices being grinded for the curry and a new word suddenly got mingled with it – kimono! Japanese kimono!

It was quite humid. Natabar was fanning himself and Bibhuprasad with a tattered palm leaf fan.

As she looked for spices inside the box, the old woman took out a beautiful thing from inside it.

"Take it, my dear," the old woman called her daughter and said, "Take this and give it to them. Why is he fanning himself with the tattered palm leaf fan?"

Sukumari came. There was a beautiful steel plate containing spices in one hand and a wonderful fine thing in the other. A shining, golden case about six inches long.

"What's this?" Natabar was slightly taken aback and indicated at the case, "What's this animal? Are you sure that a Japanese snake won't jump on me like the other day?"

"No, no …." Pressing the corner of her sari to her mouth in order to check her laughter, Sukumari said, "How can you tell such a lie! When had a snake jumped on you?"

Natabar burst into laughter. Bibhuprasad too joined in that beautiful and innocent mirth – it all seemed to be a family affair.

Sukumari blushed. Perhaps she could understand what Natabar was hinting at. Her face was coloured. A hint of artificial anger combined with reddening of the cheeks. Placing the plate of spices and the Japanese ladies' fan near Natabar, she disappeared into the darkness – away from light.

Natabar pulled the thread hanging from a corner of the fan and it opened – on its own – like the feathers of a peacock, and in no time, there was an enormous amount of cool fragrance in the hot breeze of the summer evening. The fragrance of sandalwood! The fan was made of a few fine blades of sandalwood.

"Wonderful! What a beautiful fragrance!" Bibhuprasad was overwhelmed. He was ecstatic.

The old woman was cutting the vegetables carried from the village with a knife. She was listening to the accolades showered by Natabar and Bibhuprasad.

"Sukumari's mother has made this in her own hand ... did you know that? Everything except the case is handmade. Look! What fine workmanship has gone into making these blades! This is what she is capable of! Not only this! You would come to know if she stayed here for some days – she is a musician and you cannot leave these people if her voice ever got inside your system. She plays the mridangam and harmonium. I used to go to their house in my childhood to leather the drum of the mridangam. I came to know these people then. These are all strange tales ... I'll tell you about them later. Her husband is in a ship ... he was a sweeper ... but he has received a series of promotions and now works as a mate ... I'll tell you later about all these things ...."

The old woman could perhaps hear Natabar's words; but she kept herself busy in cooking, not wanting to hear them overtly.

The tinkling sound of utensils made of steel and china clay, the narration of Natabar, the conversation between Sukumari and her mother, the hissing of refrigerators from the potato godown nearby, the lowing of the cow in the cowshed of the contractor and that marvelous fragrance on top of everything else ... Bibhuprasad was slowly returning to his childhood ... he too had a mother some day. An evening like this ... it got quite late in the night when arrangements were made for preparations of cakes and sweets the night before some festival. Conversation flowed, *paans* were made, the fragrance of cakes moved in the air, light banter continued … his father helped his mother make those cakes, the kids dozed momentarily and came out of slumber intermittently … they could smell all those fragrances even in their half-asleep state … Aniruddha was quite small; he came awake suddenly. He stared uncomprehendingly; shook his legs and smiled inside his tiny, rotund cheeks. He was about six or seven months old! The whole family gathered around the baby. Her mother sang lullabies from within clenched teeth. It was the dead of the night. A cow lowed in the neighbour's cowshed … this was exactly an evening like that!

They woke Bibhuprasad up from a light sleep. The plates had been laid. Bibhuprasad and Natabar sat together to eat. Bibhuprasad noticed that the beautiful china plate had been laid for him – the esteemed guest of the evening, Bibhuprasad.

Cancer had been taken by surprise – there was no place for poverty, uncertainties and death in the domestic environment of that wonderful evening!

FIFTEEN

But the night – especially the middle of the night! A time when the eyes failed to work – what worked was the box just behind the eyes – imagination! Imagination was trying to hide inside a warm nest hanging in a concealed branch of a high, invulnerable tree and was failing to do so. It slipped every time – down and down – to the uncertain, troubled world – the night was a trying time like that for loving, optimistic people.

Bibhuprasad woke up hearing the muffled sobbing of Natabar.

"Natabar! Natabar! What's happening to you?" Bibhuprasad sat up.

The two of them were sleeping near each other. The fan was moving over them. There was a slight chill. They were sleeping on two classroom benches. There was only a pillow each under their heads. They hid the pillows inside a cupboard in the laboratory during the day time and came to sleep in the laboratory in the nights after finishing dinner. There was a small room adjacent to the laboratory. They studied there during their M.Sc. days. They studied in the room during the day time, worked in the laboratory and slept in the college during the nights. Not just these two – the college building provided shelter for many other poor, homeless students. They made something of themselves after passing out. Some constructed their own homes to find a bit of shelter. There were others who depended on that one room throughout their lives. Natabar and Bibhuprasad – the two friends suffering the same fate – had also found the same place. There was no other place for them in this world.

As they left their house, Natabar warned Sukumari, "Be careful! Don't open the door in the night if anyone calls."

Sukumari's mother answered for her, "Son! Don't worry about us. Both of you go and sleep. It's quite late at night. You'll leave for work early in the morning. Sleep peacefully. What are we afraid of? We've spent our entire life by ourselves. Why should we be afraid when we don't have anything with us?"

Natabar and Bibhuprasad left. However, Natabar reminded the old woman again, "Aunty! This is not the village. It is the city. Anything might happen here and you won't get any wiser. I am warning you because of that. Don't misunderstand me."

Those were the days when the city was rocking because of incidents like the murder of a woman called Shantilata and some such events. It was a gamble for poor and lower middle class families to live in the city with women and kids. A girl leaves for school in the morning; no one knows whether she will return home in the evening. A jeep would stop at your door in the middle of the night. The jeep or car of some contractor or rich boy fond of hunting. Your wife – the mother of your child – would open the door to find her lost jewel. The girl's eyes would be dilated and fixed amid a bundle of cloth and a sea of blood. The mouth would be opening and shutting. There would be no language in this world to understand the pain of her dry mouth. That would be the gift for the mother of a poor or lower middle class family in the society of this age. And she has to take it in her stride.

The nasal voice of Natabar chilled Bibhuprasad even more – more than the chillness of the atmosphere.

"No, nothing," answered Natabar. I was only dreaming about my father. His goiter is the same still ... it hasn't got any better." Bibhuprasad was lost in thought for a while. He didn't feel the necessity of explaining things to someone who had just lost his mother by telling him something off the cuff.

Natabar sat up. He took a walk outside. The shadows of a few tall and dense trees standing opposite the street lights had stretched inside the college building. Bibhuprasad could not sleep any longer. He wanted to open the laboratory and work through the rest of the night. He took out the key to the laboratory from under his pillow.

But Natabar stopped him and said, "Listen! I've a great deal to talk to you. I'll leave for the hospital in the morning and you'll be busy somewhere. I have to discuss something important with you. Come, let's go. We'll sit on the cement benches beside the playground and talk – for the night. And, after that ...." He kept quiet for a while and said, "After that – we may have to go our own separate ways in the morning!"

Bibhuprasad tried to make sense of Natabar's words. He had guessed earlier – the boiling stream of lava flowing under the hard and relatively cool exterior of Natabar had not died down yet. He had perhaps become a bit subdued only because of the influence of that girl named Sukumari.

The two of them crossed the road and reached the playground. They sat down on a clean bench. Bibhuprasad looked up and saw the street lights reflecting from those golden fringes of the sunari flowers hanging down from the trees.

A fragrance ran through the mind of Bibhuprasad

for one thousandth part of a second – Murasha! Then it vanished of its own. Just the way it had come without any rhyme or reason.

Natabar had been sitting quietly. As if he was getting ready like a time bomb.

Bibhuprasad felt tired after a while and pinched Natabar on the arm and said, "Hey! Did you call me here to sit quietly like this? Why don't you say something? What's biting you? Come on; get the poison out of your system!"

Natabar still kept quiet.

Bibhuprasad could understand that silence of Natabar. He was not ready as yet perhaps. His confused thoughts had not taken any concrete shape yet – like the indefinite, passing clouds of summer.

Natabar blurted out suddenly, "Bibhu, can't you arrange a loan of five hundred rupees for me – a cash loan?

Bibhuprasad was stunned. Trying to focus on Natabar's face in the dim light, he said, "Cash? Five hundred?"

Natabar was again lost in his own world.

Bibhuprasad smiled a bit and said, "Good! You've reminded me of something. I don't have a dime with me. I had thought of asking you for a loan tomorrow morning – a paltry fifty rupees!" Bibhuprasad said the last few words somewhat sarcastically.

Natabar came to his senses. He had perhaps forgotten about the money that he had borrowed from Bibhuprasad while leaving for his village. The words of Bibhuprasad lashed Natabar like a whip.

"Bibhuprasad!" Natabar was angry, "At times, a cruel Shylock works within you. Had I called you here today to get a reminders about your loan?"

"Natabar!" Bibhuprasad was amazed at this extreme

sensitiveness of his friend. He had absolutely no intention of hurting him, but –

Natabar stood up – as if he was getting ready to run away or to strangle Bibhuprasad in the middle of that lonely playground.

"Natabar! You're behaving like a spoilt kid! Come and sit. I'm telling you – why do you get ruffled so easily? You'll ruin your health this way. We're scientists. There should be some kind of logic in our words and deeds. Why do you become so emotional? Sit down! Tell me what's biting you."

Bibhuprasad was consoling Natabar.

But Natabar …!

"Don't try to be too clever, Bibhuprasad! You think that you're a saint. You never lose your equanimity. The reason is you have a father to back you up. And you've a tongue in your mouth too – that can lick anyone's feet without any objection – any insult, vilification or smear campaign. But do you think that everyone is a slave and a bootlicker in this world?" he answered.

Bibhuprasad's tiredness vanished. He could know that the image that was standing before him and trying to inflame him was not Natabar. He was the ghost of that 'camel hair cap' of Natabar! Natabar – the son of Lord William Bentick; but Bibhuprasad kept quiet. He gave a chance to Natabar to vomit the poison and cleanse his system.

"Do you know who I discover within you at times?" Natabar said in a malicious voice, "I know – there's hardly anything to choose between Manmohan and you. Both of you are opportunists – rich and middle class! You can change colour like a chameleon in no time. I know you guys. I know you very well from the day you guys got together to get me bashed up in the fruit market!"

"We got you beaten up?" Bibhuprasad opposed in a feeble voice.

"Sure! Who else? Just because they didn't get fish to eat, they instigated people who didn't get rice to eat shouting from the rooftops that the Na'Anka Famine has arrived yet again. Who were those people? Did they not belong to rich and middle class families like you? Those who demand a day's pay of a labourer for a dozen bananas – who suck the blood of a day labourer for a seer of rice. And what do they give in return? Those who throw five rupees and buy the vote of a working class man for five years. Don't you belong to them – is this not your real identity? Manmohan and you?"

"Me?"

"Yes, yes, you!" And, suddenly, Natabar came back to his goal and, in his usual manner, charged Bibhuprasad directly, "I know, Bibhuprasad – you've lied to me. I'm myself going through a tough period in my life. Still, when I'm trying to save a vulnerable family by running constantly to the hospital, how can you lie to me while you have five hundred rupees in your pass book? And that too when it's a question of life and death? Do you have any idea? A single day may prove fatal for a cancer patient. Don't you feel any pity? Don't you have an inclination to save the life of a wonderful woman? You do not know; you still do not know the cockles of that heart, Bibhuprasad – you do not know anything."

Natabar's voice was getting feeble again. It was again filled with grief and regret.

But what about Bibhuprasad? Bibhuprasad's whole being seemed to crumble. No, it was not the sarcasm of Natabar; it was his own conscience biting him.

Bibhuprasad had indeed tried to forget until then

that five hundred rupees had been stashed away in a corner of his house as a hidden treasure typically like a clever, quick-witted member of a middle class family. Two weeks ago, he had received six hundred rupees from the college office as his research scholarship for six months. He had paid fifty rupees out of that to Natabar and deposited the rest in the post office – for future contingencies! The future that had been staring at him with hideous eyes with the impending retirement of his father – for that future.

Bibhuprasad was terribly distressed with the harsh criticism of Natabar. He had never thought that Natabar was capable of envying the resources of another equally poor person set aside for a long, indefinite voyage. But that was the test of friendship!

Bibhuprasad was scared. He felt as if a famine-stricken crowd pursued him in order to barge into his house and snatch away his food bowl!

"Remember, Bibhuprasad!" Natabar warned him again, "I'm not asking this money for myself or for the mother of Sukumari! I'm asking this money for a responsible and conscientious servant of the country – for a doctor, who needs some compensation beyond his salary in order to consider his responsibilities to be his responsibilities. I want to buy some affection, sympathy and a special sense of duty from the 'fruit' market of today by paying this money – just as I had bought some apples and oranges for my dead mother with the help of your money – using up twenty rupees in the process."

And Natabar paid Bibhuprasad back in his own coin. He seemed satiated after that and felt quiet.

"Why do you attack me, Natabar? What have I done to you? I've helped you in the past to the best of my ability and will also do the same in future. But do you think you would be able to extract affection, sympathy and love from someone forcibly in this manner? You're on the wrong track, my dear friend! You won't get any nectar if you follow this path – you would only get poison! There would only be bloodshed in the end!" Bibhuprasad finally said, not being able to contain himself any longer.

But, Natabar shot back, "When one would not have the money in his pocket to buy your nectar, he would be forced to shed blood in order to buy it!"

Bibhuprasad lost his cool. Not able to take the diatribe any longer, he said, "Natabar! You're talking like a communist!"

Finally, there was a smile on Natabar's lips. He softened somewhat and came and sat on the bench near Bibhuprasad. He said jokingly, "Don't get scared … I'm not going to kill you. I remember you – you're Bibhuprasad, my friend – who has stood by me in my misfortune, who has provided me with shelter and who has shared my happiness and grief. How could I kill you? No way … but remember I get my five hundred rupees from you with the first rays of the sun tomorrow!"

"Natia!' Bibhuprasad laughed upon hearing that jocular voice. He said in the usual language of their studentship days, "Hey! You're worse than any Bihari thug! You want to be known as a great philanthropist by robbing Peter to pay Paul! Hey! Which is more valuable? The future of a poor research scholar or the life of an elderly, rustic woman? You'll take my money and pay it to the doctor. But can you guarantee that the woman will survive? From the clutches of a disease like cancer at that?"

But it was another challenge for Natabar. He answered enthusiastically, "If capital can guarantee the Nobel Prize for a research scholar, his ultimate ambition, then capital can also guarantee the life of a human being!"

With that one sentence, they leaned towards each other, and experienced the warmth of each other's hand in that darkness, and Natabar's enthusiasm again got the better of him. He had forgotten the dream of his father by that time, in exchange of which, he had gained the friendship of Bibhuprasad.

"Ah1 How beautiful are the fringes of this goldmohur! Listen! A cuckoo is whistling! Morning is in the offing. What a soothing breeze! Look at the blue light coming from that house in the distance and listen again – the sound of the train on the bridge! I just love this part of the night!"

Bibhuprasad had done his best to get Natabar in a mellow mood. He was pulling Natabar from man to nature only to return again to man through the path of nature.

Natabar and Bibhuprasad – Bibhuprasad and Bhabaniprasad. Their proportional properties could be best understood by framing an algebraic equation. Bibhuprasad stood now near Natabar the same way as Bhabaniprasad had stood near his son the other day.

The sharp tongue of Natabar had softened quite a bit by that time. Instead of thinking about death, he had started thinking about life.

"I had also written poetry like you in my childhood." Bibhuprasad had helped Natabar in reflecting childhood in his voice. That voice of his! It was as if Bibhuprasad was getting himself expressed in that voice – more clearly than Natabar himself!

"I was perhaps in class nine or ten when I fell in love for the first time!"

Bibhuprasad buttoned his shirt carefully. A strong breeze had started blowing. Summer breeze.

"They were staying about two miles away from our village – on the bank of the river where I waited for a boat everyday – on my way to the school. I discovered my first lover when I looked at the deep blue water of the river and learnt to lose myself. Do you know who that was? It was a tree! That tree was the first indication of my poetic bent of mind! That tree was like a strange, romantic dream! A Japanese tree – whose reflection made me lose myself in the blue mirror of the river.

"I got acquainted with that well-to-do family living near the river through that tree. The tree was beautiful like a chintz kimono-clad girl. Mahana, the sweeper – I had told you that he worked on a ship – he was not at home at the time. Sukumari was about seven or eight years old. And her mother …."

It was not in the least difficult for Bibhuprasad to recognize that voice of Natabar. He was as attentive as a musician – to translate the waves of the voice into the feelings of the heart, and all of a sudden, Bibhuprasad translated those feelings into words, "I know, Bibhuprasad!" In order to make light of Natabar's flowing emotions, Bibhuprasad said, "I know who you are in love with. She's not Sukumari. She's neither the melody of the river nor the strange Japanese tree. She's this woman – Sukumari's mother! She must be gorgeously beautiful in her young days … beautiful like a river! So, what do you say?"

Natabar picked up Bibhuprasad's hand and pressed it hard. That was a tacit admission.

"Speak in that case! Spill the beans! I'll give you one more opinion of mine about you after that," said Bibhuprasad like a judge.

"Listen then! Right from the beginning!" Natabar leaned back against the cement bench. Swaying in the breeze, the flowers from the gulmohar tree fell on them. Natabar started, "Those were terrible days when my father had left the jatra party and lived in the village. He had returned home, afflicted with goiter. His reign in the jatras was over. He spoke in a guttural voice and his face was a sight. He had trimmed his lustrous, long hair and only had a ponytail. It's about those days.

"There was a severe drought that year. There was a terrible shortage of food. It was as bad as a famine. The gold and silver medals of my father had started going one by one over to the wooden treasury of the ration shop owned by the village landlord.

"I was once first in the hundred metre dash in the sports competition held in our school. The president of the function was a gentleman from Cuttack – quite a famous man. At the award giving ceremony, the landlord, who was present there, declared that he would present a few medals to the winners. The medals were hung around our necks when we went to get our prizes. When the president hung a medal around my neck, I discovered that it belonged to my father!

"I felt as if I had been hit by a stinging arrow. That day, I saw how our medals were being distributed one by one – courtesy of the landlord! The landlord sat arrogantly and smiled through the corners of his lips as the president awarded the medals and looked at him with appreciative eyes.

"Finally, the time came for the presidential address. The president started, 'Brothers and sisters, you all know that today's child will lead the nation tomorrow. He will be the leader ….'"

"An incident had taken place that morning," Natabar's narration suddenly took a different turn. "There was a clamour about cleaning the commode of the honourable people who had come from Cuttack. One gentleman had carried a commode with him from Cuttack. There was no toilet in our school. The headmaster had asked the boys of the school to dig a hole the day before. The hole had been covered on all sides and was to be used as a makeshift latrine. But, for some reason, the gentleman used his commode instead of using the makeshift latrine. A sweeper was needed after that; but there was no sweeper around! Sukumari's people were the only sweepers in our village. But Mahana was not there. His wife was summoned … this old woman that you see."

Natabar was lost in thought for a while. He wiped his nose with his handkerchief. Then he thought of something, and, glancing at the Gulmohar flowers and the early morning sky, he said, "India was already independent by then."

Natabar stood up and brushed off the gulmohar petals on his head, he said again, "Not just independence. Mahatma Gandhi had already been assassinated by then."

Then he sat down and started again, "She was Mahana's wife. She sold perfumes at the time. Traders used to buy perfumes and scented oil from her to sell in the market. Mahana always carried back a few cans of perfume with him whenever he returned from abroad. He moved around Japan, China, Philippines, Java, Sumatra and a host of other countries. He always smuggled in a few products from those countries when he returned home. He even brought watches, cameras and transistor radios – we saw all those things in his house in our childhood even though they were beyond the means of more well-to-do people of the village. Anyway, all these are beside the point."

Natabar gulped. He pulled in a long breath and started again, "The situation took a different turn when Mahana's wife refused to clean the commode. As a result, the honourable person from Cuttack concluded that the people of the village had deliberately insulted him. He got angry and summoned the landlord – the landlord was the union president at the time.

"Union president – one who is known as the sarpanch these days.

"The landlord called the people and informed, 'Listen to me, all of you! There would be no supplies of ration to this area from tomorrow if the commode is not cleaned by ten this morning.'

"'No ration from tomorrow? Clothes, sugar, kerosene – nothing would be available?' People stared at the union president for a long while. That was the time when the First Five Year Plan had just been initiated. The rationing of commodities in force at the time of war had been eased temporarily only to be reimposed with greater force.

"Anyway, the commode of the honourable person was cleaned before ten by a teacher who had received basic training. He took advantage of the situation. The trained teacher picked up the bucket and vanished even before the word was out of the mouth of the landlord. The reputation of the village as also the union president, which was at stake because of the arrogance of Mahana's wife, was salvaged. Anyway, forget it – it's a different story. The prize-giving ceremony was over.

"But, when I returned home and talked about my exploits on the field, I saw my father breaking into a sob.

"I saw how an old man was sitting in a corner of the verandah like a ball of meat ignored by everyone – that was my father! Once upon a time, he was the king of the jatras in the whole of India! And this is what he got at the far end of his life!

"My mother had taken the medal from me to examine it even as my father was sobbing silently. I knew she would have sent me out with the medal in an hour and said, "Go and get some tea, sugar and kerosene from the landlord's shop."

"I was exhausted both mentally and physically after slugging throughout the day in the school sports. I told mother, 'Ma! I'm terribly hungry. Give me something to eat.'

"And it was as if my fate came out to ridicule me in the shape of my mother!

"In a while, I saw my mother open the medal from the corner of her sari to hand it over to me and said, 'Take this! Get some rice. You'll have something to eat when the rice is cooked!' This was my mother, Bibhuprasad. I had never seen another person as harsh as her. She had thrown the medal at me that day and had said that – making an ominous insinuation.

"'I've been telling you!' she shouted at me angrily in her usual rustic, cynical woman's voice, 'I've been telling this accursed family repeatedly – we should have nothing to do with jatras, we don't need school education and so forth. Will it fill our stomachs – this goddamned school education! I've been telling these degenerates – throw those damned books away. Take the plough in your hand. Work as a day labourer – the farmer's son won't starve. What would we do with these medals?'

"Then there were many other things ….

"I ran away from home throwing that first medal that I had won in the first hundred meter dash of my life at my mother.

"I had been drained out. I walked towards the river. That was the last refuge of the people in that area to set all physical and mental hunger at rest for all time to come!

Natabar's voice suddenly died down. Bibhuprasad was startled. A train was passing on the Kathjodi Bridge with a deafening noise. Natabar started again, "The river was overfull with water. Depthless. Full of crocodiles.

"I sat on the bank with my legs stretched down. Unfathomable water had raised its head like a black cobra twenty feet below my feet. It had invited me several times earlier. I discovered those others there – those who had gone there before me on the invitation of that black cobra. A school kid had gone there six months back after failing the examination. A young man of the village had gone there earlier suffering from an incurable disease. Many others were there too. They had gone there having lost the battle of life. Life had supposedly betrayed them! I had been sitting there looking at the faces of those defeated people in the liquid darkness below my feet.

"I had no idea about the time. The sky was getting lit slowly. I lifted my head and looked up at the sky. The moon was rising – just about rising. It was the dark fortnight. I was a bit startled looking at the sky, the moon and the water below (I wrote poetry looking at this one day) and the strange, lonely environment around me. Was it not natural to get a bit startled?

"Shall I really go away? Have I come here to leave this world? I asked myself and then I started shivering uncontrollably for some reason.

"Staring far towards the village, I discovered that the building of the landlord seemed to be rising into the sky against the background of an open sky – like a temple!

"I had continued to sit like that. All of a sudden, I felt

as if I was a 'Dharama' and that temple far away that was being kissed by moonlight – that building of the landlord – that was my creation … 'the Konark'! Built with the blood of my nation!

"I came to my senses.

"No, I'm not stupid – I'm not a stupid childlike Dharama! Before they kill me, I'll tell this world who has built this Konark and who actually deserves the honour for its creation. I revolted inside me. I rose. I rose, Bibhuprasad – the way I had never risen – I had never discovered myself within me earlier!

"Three days later –

"A mysterious incident shook that area. The police ran from their outposts. There was a sea of people in front of the house of Mahana, the sweeper. A young Harijan boy was discovered in the backyard of Mahana's house in a severely injured state. His skull had broken open and one of his hands had multiple fractures. The police sent the young man to the doctor and started searching Mahana's house.

"Mahana's house was searched in the presence of the public. But nothing objectionable was found there. Then the police went forth to arrest Mahana's wife. The complaints against her were that she was responsible for prostitution, sale of illicit liquor and social unrest, and above all, for the imminent death of that scheduled caste boy discovered in her backyard.

"The school was closed that day in the midafternoon. Everyone had been running towards Mahana's house.

"I still remember that scene …."

Natabar stood up again. He brushed off the sunari flowers on his head and shirt. Bibhuprasad shifted position on the bench. A few bats snarled from the side of the botanical garden. The cool bridge of the last part of the night had been filled with the fragrance of lavender or some such flowers.

But Natabar continued to stand.

Bibhuprasad observed that image of Natabar. That shaven head of his; a man had been standing in front of him like a mountain of silver. Like a fiery image. It was not possible to observe his gaze in the darkness; but every word of his sounded like the report of a crumbling hill on the horizon! The cautiousness of a tiger was discernible in every movement of his limbs.

Natabar started his narration again, "I remember still. How she stood under the tree – the Japanese tree in their garden! No, no! She had not been standing there. She had been lying in wait like a lioness. Sukumari was just a kid then. She had been standing holding on to a corner of her mother's sari. Of course, she was weeping looking at all those people and the police. But her mother! I had never seen anything resembling that live image of a woman in the act of killing Mahishasura, the demon!

"The people had been waiting silently.

"A police constable was the first person to approach her with a handcuff. People were still quiet. The wife of Mahana, the sweeper versus the police or the government! Who could intervene!

"Brother! She had been lying in wait until then – that image of Durga riding the lion. The police were closing in. And, do you know, Bibhuprasad – what happened after that? No, no! You cannot even imagine. Perhaps you've never locked your eyes with the fiery image of Shakti! She had gathered a staff from some place in the meantime and she was swinging it! Just like a man swinging a staff! When she made a charge towards the police, I remember very well, someone seemed to wake me up from sleep and said in my ears, 'Come running! Get my blessings! Gratify me, you son of Ola Raut – I'll get the whole world to serve you like dogs!' I don't know if anyone else heard her words at the time.

"Mahana's wife was shouting, 'Be careful! I'm a woman. I'll bash the skull of anyone who dares touch me – just the way I bashed the skull of that fellow in the backyard! Bloody sons of bitches! What do you take me to be? You're frightening me because I'm a woman? You do not know me, you rascals! Aren't you ashamed of yourselves? The whole village has assembled here to get one woman! Is this your justice? Is this what your government is paying you for? You've no shame! Is this the government of Gandhi Mahatma?'

"The onlookers started whispering among themselves all of a sudden. There was a slight indication that the crowd had a conscience after all even though it lacked a thinking faculty.

"A school teacher stood up and asked the police, 'You've come to arrest a woman. Do you have an arrest warrant?'

"The police seemed to be a little bit on the back foot.

"But another man came out of the crowd and confronted the poor teacher, 'Sir, how many times have you come here? In the dead of the night? That woman has opened a brothel here. She has already destroyed hundreds of people ....'

"It was known to everyone that the fellow was a henchman of the landlord. Hence, no one wanted to confront him immediately. The poor teacher found himself to be all alone.

"That strange incident occurred exactly at that time. Sukumari's mother got possessed. She threw the staff away and started dancing. She continued to dance nonstop until she resembled the image of a yogin. Radiance was emitting from her firm and muscular body exposed in the process of dancing with gay abandon. That ultimate transformation of the woman – Banadurga – the image of Shakti!

"And, then the crowd came alive. The crowd had waited until then like a eunuch!

"Someone came and passed on two canes. Incense sticks, earthen lamps, pitchers, black sari, turmeric water, cocks, he-goats … everything seemed to assemble as if by magic!

"Banadurga kept on dancing.

"Some time passed in this manner. The crowd joined her in dancing for a while. The policemen were standing. The crowd had forgotten about the police then.

"And, what happened after that? Exactly what happens in such cases everywhere. Revolution! Yes, yes – it was the same thing – revolution! A revolution started like the French or Russian Revolution – marching! Banadurga was in front. And the crowd followed – like a faithful dog!

"They went first to the Gramadevati – to offer prayers.

"But the leader was still dancing.

"It was as if she was a sea of energy and a storm had risen in that sea that day!

"But the procession didn't stop there that day – near the image of Gramadevati. The procession went straight – in one direction now.

"We knew by that time what was going to happen that day – what novel revolution was going to start that day.

"In a little while, they stopped at the target – in front of the house of the landlord.

"The Possessed made the proclamation. The

Possessed shouted out her order, 'Let Giridhari Sahoo, the son of Hari Sahoo, be presented!'

"It didn't take long. Giridhari Sahoo, the landlord, presented himself humbly before Banadurga.

"It didn't take very long either for the poor landlord to be present before that wonderful people's court and to admit everything before that half-divine judge with folded hands … to recount all his deeds one after another … Giridhari Sahoo, the landlord, blabbered everything right from the beginning of the Creation.

"That was perhaps the first trial of the century in the people's court where there was no need for evidence, proof, law, precedence, advocate, opposite party, cross examination, etc. The police was standing – like an image of stone in a museum.

"The landlord had continued to blabber nonstop! A simple, uncomplicated and open heart – like a child.

"'Mother! Mother! Save me! Save me!' The union president was hallucinating at intervals after being flogged repeatedly by that metaphysical cane.

"And he was making new admissions every time –

"'Mother, I've looked at my brother's wife with lust ….'

"'Mother, I've looked furtively at my daughter-in-law a couple of times!'

"'Mother, I've adulterated one seer of oil to sell it as three seers!'

"'Mother, I had passed off sand while selling sugar to the blind mother of Kinei Bhoi in my childhood!'

"'With a bribe of ten bags of fine rice, half a pitcher of pure ghee and various other things, I had got the permit of Madhu Sahoo cancelled for the ration shop.'

"'Last summer, I paid people to set fire to the Harijan

colony as they had voted against me when I contested for the post of union president'

"And his blabbering continued for some time. It was a long list.

"And it finally came to an end when the landlord opened his 'black' godown with his own hand. People returned home – with a bagful of rice on the back and mark of vermillion on their foreheads – a few of them also had the marks of canes on their backsides.

"And the wife of Mahana, the sweeper was accepted to be not guilty for all time to come since that day. The police was no longer seen after that.

"And this was the woman to whose house we went in our childhood to get various odd jobs done. I remember that voice of hers. When she sang, her voice became one with the voice of the river that flowed beyond the greenery surrounding her house.

"I could sing mellifluously in my childhood. I remember the day I was singing that song from the collection of poems by Gopalkrishna –

'When I had been to Kalindasuta for water
I got what I deserved, my friend ....'
"For me, she was a jewel with a thousand faces, looking at whose numerous faces, a man discovered his numerous reflections ... each one different from the other ... that was the identity of the woman ...."

SIXTEEN

Yet another storm had lashed the tea club of the department in the meantime. Bibhuprasad went to the tea club that day after getting the bad news – to enquire about the matter.

But an unexpected anger and apprehension brewed in his mind that day when he entered inside the tea club, as a result of which, he totally forgot the bad news about which he had gone to enquire.

Basically, the bad news was like this. A rumour was suddenly making the rounds that the third son of Mr. Sethi had also died in some accident. When he heard about the incident, Bibhuprasad was so distressed that he felt as if the gods had cursed Mr. Sethi or perhaps the entire burden of the countrywide sacrifice needed for the economic planning of the country at the time had fallen on his shoulders. When plans were being made to prevent deaths occurring due to starvation and malnutrition by gathering whatever capital was available in the country and using it for the development of agriculture, the Sethi Family had lost its first two children by way of requiting the 'Satan's share' – in the incident of poisonous food. And when planning demanded the development of heavy industry in place of agriculture and wanted the 'Satan's share' again according to its unalterable divine rule, the third child of the Sethi Family could not also ignore the demands of planning. As the kid looked inside a drum of boiling coaltar out of curiosity while returning from the school, the drum overturned and the kid was lost inside that boiling coaltar forever.

But the problem being discussed that day in the tea club was even more important. Bibhuprasad became aware of the more agonizing event of the day upon looking at the way they were sipping their tea and glancing at the pierced wings of their frightened eyes. They were sipping their tea quietly. And they were silently reciting –

"Here comes the storm

Pay your respects, friend …."

Of course, the storm was not about the death of the third child of the Sethi Family. Manmohan was again at the centre of the storm this time.

The sensational success of Manmohan was the topic of the silent discussion taking place that day. The matter was that a research paper on Manmohan under the guidance of Dr. Sharma had been published in one of the most reputed journals of the world. Dr. Sharma happened to be the research guide of Mr. Sethi. A rumour was going around that the paper had not been written by Manmohan! It was Mr. Sethi's paper.

As he returned from the department to his house, Bibhuprasad had perhaps forgotten the ultimate sacrifice of Mr. Sethi for the nation. Only that one line was playing in his mind –

'Here comes the storm.'

SEVENTEEN

As such unfortunate incidents occurred at the highest level of intelligentsia of the university, Bibhuprasad too was not conscious about the earthquake that had taken place in the political arena of the state along with others

But the entire city had come alive that morning!

Election – 196-!

Election!

The election that came regularly to this country as a political periodic fever. It came to the cottage of democracy like a flood in a river. It came as a famine of the last century to this Utkal – to the cottage of arts!

But this election was different from all other elections. It proved to be a traumatic beginning especially for the inhabitants of 'Niraba Nilaya'.

The old woman had been transferred to the hospital for the past to five days. With his own eyes, Bibhuprasad had seen how critical the relative speed of time could be for a cancer patient.

But the surgery had not been performed on the old woman until then. The money promised by Bibhuprasad had not as yet been withdrawn from the post office because of certain unforeseen situation.

But the cancer had gone on spreading without waiting for the post office. And, Natabar's sulking had gone on increasing with every passing day. But Bibhuprasad was undone. It was not as if he neglected to run to the post office every day. But the post office ran along its own path without bothering for cancer just the way cancer had gone on increasing without bothering to wait for the post office!

The first day was a Saturday. When Bibhuprasad presented the pass book on reaching the counter at 12 noon, the pass book was pushed back to him with a silent finger pointing in one direction. Bibhuprasad looked in that direction and discovered a notice proclaiming the rule in bold letters – 'All transactions closed after 12 noon'. All his entreaties fell on deaf ears after that. The next day was a Sunday. It was the second of the month when Bibhuprasad reached the counter in the first hour on Monday. Standing at the end of a long queue, he was constantly praying that his signature on the withdrawal slip would be acceptable to the clerk.

Alas!

If a day had been ordained in the fate of a cancer patient when the signature was to be rejected, then this was the day!

Reclaiming the pass book and the withdrawal slip from the counter, Bibhuprasad tried to reach the counter once again. But he had to get back to the end of the long queue again when he could sense a revolt brewing among the crowd. The Rule!

Time didn't wait for anyone. And, both time and cancer were the two hands of a clock.

Natabar became impatient when Bibhuprasad failed to withdraw the money in the first three days. He developed doubts about Bibhuprasad's motives – for his deliberate delay.

Natabar himself accompanied Bibhuprasad to the post office the next day; but there was no respite that day either. Natabar saw for himself that Bibhuprasad's signature did not tally with his specimen signature. Bibhuprasad was startled to see that strange expression on Natabar's face for the first time then.

Natabar's face shone at the time like a stone smeared all over with vermillion. He was forced to show some 'tact', apprehending that Natabar might do something foolhardy like the day of the picketing in front of the fruit stall.

It was a time like that – winning over the unruly cancer somehow by tact – those were the days when one had to learn how to survive one more day. The successful application of economic theory of those days lay in gaining insight into proper investment of money rather than earning it. This 'tact' had been christened as an 'unfailing weapon' in the field of political administration.

Hence, Bibhuprasad was immensely proud of himself when he counted four hundred and ninety rupees in place of five hundred rupees and handed it over to Natabar. Bibhuprasad looked at the long queue of human beings resembling a long line of ants as also the smirk on the face of the postal clerk, and said to himself silently, "Ten rupees – ten years".

The dinner of the strange family of 'Niraba Nilaya' (the name 'Chemical Cottage Industry' had perhaps been automatically forgotten since the day Sukumari had arrived) passed off amid a prehistoric, frightened silence that evening. The surgery was supposed to be conducted the next day. Natabar had met Dr. Balbrahmachari that evening with the money and the latter had apparently consoled him by saying, "There's nothing to worry about. Go in peace! Arrange the money needed for the post-operative care. Cancer has many side effects. Ordinarily, five thousand rupees is needed to take care of a cancer patient. No one knows whether the patient will live or die. But we have to take care of the patient. We should not neglect that."

Natabar had been strangely quiet that evening after returning from the hospital.

Of course, Bibhuprasad was in no mental frame to observe that explosive mental condition of Natabar. He had already done what he was expected to do. Five hundred rupees? Why? Five hundred rupees was not a small sum those days. Especially for Bibhuprasad!

However, a strange feeling of proprietorial right took its hold in the mind of Bibhuprasad when Sukumari placed the china plate before him at dinner time as on every other day. "If I have done so much for her ...." He seemed to be saying to himself.

Sukumari was serving dinner.

Losing his self-control, Bibhuprasad seemed to discover that slender hand of Sukumari for the first time that day. Two opposite streams seemed to run through his system immediately. One was like hot lava. And the other one was so contrary to it! God only knew why such a horrendous sensitiveness arose around his greedy lips! He started licking his own lips in order to perceive himself intimately once more and to make an unpleasant effort to search for his long lost entity – throughout that night.

Natabar was lost in his own world throughout the dinner. Then he left for the hospital the same night.

The surgery of the old woman was scheduled for tomorrow! Bibhuprasad had the responsibility of guarding Sukumari that night!

X X X X X

Sukumari was perhaps already asleep. Of course, her room was locked from inside. Bibhuprasad was supposed to stand guard that night. Hence, he had slept outside on a charpoy. He could not sleep. Knowingly or unknowingly, he seemed to be waiting for some clear or unclear signal!

He sat up suddenly hearing footsteps outside. He could easily recognize the man when he coughed lightly. He was no one else but his well-wisher and father's friend – Basudev, the owner of the hotel.

Bibhuprasad felt apprehensive on seeing the man come to him so late in the night. A cold sweat ran through him.

A tangent light from the contractor's house fell on a corner of the verandah. Bibhuprasad pulled the charpoy there. Basudev came on the verandah and sat on the charpoy. Then he asked, "Have you heard about the old man?"

Bibhuprasad felt as if an electric shock went through him. He almost shrieked, "What did you say? Old man? Are you talking about my father? What's wrong with him?"

Basudev pressed his hand on Bibhuprasad's mouth and said angrily, "Hey! Why are you shouting like that? It's election time. Anyone might hear us. But I received the letter in the morning. I'm busy. I could not come earlier. But do you have any idea about the conspiracies behind this? Have I not told you about this for a long time? But you chose to sit at home without doing anything. Do you know? Do you know that brat in our village who passed I.A. privately this year? He's the fellow who's coming as the headmaster – in place of your father! In the meantime, there are conspiracies going on to make sure that your father does not get any extension. That brat has got an uncle somewhere here. Apart from that, the head clerk of the office had come to the village a couple of months back
....

"Whatever you might say that fellow is really intelligent. He doesn't sit at home doing nothing like you brothers. Now, listen to me! If that fellow tied two rohus of two seers each on the cycle carrier of the head clerk, you too could have done likewise. The matter would have been closed if you could have hung a couple of hilsas in front of the cycle. The fellow would have been at a loss to know what to do. We would have seen after that – whether he would have looked in front or at the back. But you didn't do anything. And now the old man is sulking. Here, take the letter and see what he has written!"

Pushing the letter into Bibhuprasad's hand in the dim light, Basudev went on his chatter, "The old man has written out of bitter disappointment, 'Will these people dump me like this while you people are around? Why, everyone gets extension in this world! What's wrong with me? Have I become old?' Who else can the old man talk to if not to his son?"

In the dim light, Basudev opened his mouth imitating the mannerism of Bhabaniprasad and said excitedly as if he was enacting a scene in a theatre, "It's true that the old man has got all his teeth intact. But you should know! An old man is not known by his teeth or hair these days. Hadn't God said in the Bhagavad Gita to Arjuna – 'Arjuna! Do everything. But don't put emphasis on the word 'I'. Who am 'I'? Here, look inside this mouth. A galley worm is as good as a hero like you. There is no distinction here. Son, I get everything done in this world. If you think that you are the only great man around – you won't ever bend from the waist down – you can get something done without bribing or cajoling someone – forget it. No one gives a hoot about your Gandhian thought!'"

Basudev said a lot many things after that. Finally,

putting a heavy hand on Bibhuprasad's shoulder, he whispered in his ears, "Listen! Do something! You've to arrange at least five hundred rupees from somewhere if you want to save the old man. You know it's just not a job for the old man – it's his life. The order for his retirement will be dispatched from here the day after tomorrow. I've kept track of the news. There's still time for you! You can save the old man's job if you play your cards right. Just not for a year! There's a chance now. His life can be extended by another five years. Get busy! Act like a son! Everyone will say that you care about your father!"

Bibhuprasad was startled. Five hundred rupees? Exactly five hundred rupees again? The shadow of the mango tree in the contractor's house looked darker than ever. Basudev's face had been lost in that darkness. There was a trace of a smile on his face as if he was testing Bibhuprasad.

Finding Bibhuprasad to be quiet, Basudev said angrily, "Get up, Sir! What's the use of sitting like that? Arrange the money during the night somehow. There's just a day in our hands. The order will be dispatched the day after tomorrow. You still have your father's letter in your hand. Read it! The old man hasn't borne his heart before you. But he would like you to make an effort for him ...."

"What can I do? What's there in my hand?" Bibhuprasad felt that he was being indicted for something he had not done. He tried to defend himself.

"What did you say? What's there in your hand?" Basudev gulped. Then he looked around him furtively and seemed to make a frontal attack on Bibhuprasad, "Sir, you're educated. He's the father who has brought you into this world. He made something of you making such sacrifices. When would you pay him back? In your next birth? This is not the age when the father would take ill and the son and the daughter-in-law would pay off their debt by nursing him. As such, you educated people have eradicated diseases. A person might fall ill only once in a blue moon and so the children would hardly have the chance of serving the parents. And the kind of diseases that afflict people now – no one has any control over those. They will just kill. We would be in hardly any position to do anything for such diseases; the doctors and nurses would take over. But they too won't do anything! Who bothers for whom these days, Sir? Pay money on the one hand and get your medicine on the other. Listen to a word of reassurance!

"Listen to me. Do as I say. Get me five hundred rupees somehow by tomorrow morning. Two things can be simultaneously achieved by that. Your father will benefit and I'll benefit too."

Basudev stopped for a moment. Finally, he admitted, "Listen, Sir! I'm in a great deal of trouble. You know that the election is upon us. This is not an election but a Zizia tax. Now, see. What kind of hotel am I running? But I'm supposed to pay a thousand rupees as a contribution towards the election. I've finally persuaded them to wait until tomorrow evening. My hotel would be raided by people from the sales tax, income tax and the health departments if I don't cough up the money by tomorrow. Please help me now, Sir. Let me get over this problem. And just think for a while. If I manage to get over my problem, you too get over yours – your father would benefit. Would you care to listen to me?"

Basudev was an extremely intelligent man. The general knowledge of such people was so strong that they could touch profound thoughts even while indulging in idle conversation. Basudev pushed near Bibhuprasad and whispered in an even fainter voice, "This light that you see here, Sir! Wherefrom does it come? Do you think it's coming out on its own from this rapacious contractor's house? This light has fallen here so that you and I can look at each other and talk here. Friendship will take root from this conversation. That friendship is not meaningless, Sir! You'll come to my help if there's friendship between us. If you help me, I'll help the candidates at the polling. Do you know who is contesting from our constituency? You would come to know in due course. But remember – if I pay money to their election fund, the tax people won't touch me. And do you know where they would go if they didn't come to my shop? They will go to educated idlers like you and your father who endure everything and call themselves the intelligentsia. The real juice will come out when these people are squeezed and you would finally come alive. Only after that you would open your eyes and discover for yourself what you've done to the country. Then there would be chaos. The country would only understand then about the conspiracies being hatched in that house from where this light is coming. Sit quietly for fifteen days and you will see that this house would be the centre of the country – I'm prophesying! The five hundred rupees you would give me would go through the tunnel of this light to this house. The death sentence of your father would be annulled and dispatched the day after tomorrow morning from this house. The light carries such meaning. I'm leaving. It's quite late at night. Deliver that five hundred rupees that you have in your pass book to me first thing in the morning. Nothing is hidden from me! I know it very well. You're my regular customer. Do I not know how much money you have?"

Basudev got up and left as carefully as he had come.

He had come and gone. But he left a strange experience inside the fist of Bibhuprasad behind him. Clasping the letter inside his hand with even greater force, Bibhuprasad sat through the night like a statue.

The signal of Sukumari's breathing in the adjacent room didn't bother him any longer as it had done in the evening. His only thought then was to somehow arrange five hundred rupees by the next morning and help his father keep his word like a good son.

X X X X X

It was dawn. Sukumari still hadn't opened her door. Bibhuprasad got up, the letter of his father still in his hand. Father's promise!

Bibhuprasad came out on the street. He stopped suddenly at a place after walking about two hundred paces. It was still dark. There were very few people on the road. All of a sudden, there was hammering inside his chest and his sight too was lost to him for a few moments.

When he recovered his sight, he felt that a strange force had followed him throughout his life and at times it had preceded him too.

Bibhuprasad looked around him furtively and finally stooped down to pick up the brown coloured purse wet with dew from the road and put it away under his shirt in a flash.

Next, his natural reaction was to go somewhere where he could be alone by walking gravely on some bylane as if nothing had happened. But he did something stupid. He started running as if an invisible force was chasing him from behind.

His instinct pulled him somewhere without his

knowledge. He recovered after a long time and discovered that he was in a part of the city which was not in the least familiar to him although he had lived in the city for a long twelve years.

Bibhuprasad was only looking for a place to hide until then. Of course, there was no justifiable reason for him to believe in his subconscious that that part of the city was the safest place for him to hide.

Bibhuprasad again looked around him furtively. There were people everywhere. Perhaps a meeting could be held somewhere nearby. The election was in the offing. There was excitement in the air.

Two persons came quite close to Bibhuprasad. He crossed his hands across his chest as if he was shivering in the cold. He turned back and moved to the side of the road.

The two persons went away talking to each other. He heard the biggest news of the morning from their conversation – a few high-ranking officers being suspended from service.

An elderly man was saying, "Did you see? How this matter was decided in a minute when nothing could be done through so many arguments, newspaper editorials, recriminations, public opinion and the ballot paper? No one can deal with these officers. The ministers are servile to them. Only a king would know how to control these people. You are all talking about democracy – but democracy cannot handle these officers!"

"How was all this be done if democracy could not handle anything? These high and mighty officers are out now because of democracy. There is also an I.A.S. officer among them! Proceedings are being drawn against a few more. The Chief Minister would sign the files in a day or two. It is said that the big fish have been caught in the net this time. Again, that 'rogue' Govind Das is also in this list. So, Dharma is still there in this Kalyug …!" Bibhuprasad could not hear what else the second man was saying. But he could hear the name of Manmohan's father being mentioned repeatedly in their discussion. Govind Das, the Rogue – Manmohan's father was famously known by this name.

Bibhuprasad could repeatedly hear the hammering inside his chest. The sound inside the chest was so apparent perhaps because of pressing the purse down on his chest so hard.

So, Govind Das, Manmohan's father, had been suspended! Bibhuprasad's head reeled. A building resembling a huge palace was being built on the side of the road. A lot of labourers were busy in their work. Many trucks and concrete mixers were roaring. Bibhuprasad sat down for some time. His sense of security increased manifold amid so many people and the roar of the machines.

Bibhuprasad called a passing labourer to him all of a sudden. His throat was parched by that time. He was feeling a lot of pain in his two hands by that time. Perhaps there was very little circulation of blood in them as he had kept his hands pressed to his chest for such a long time.

Bibhuprasad felt his entire body numb. He again said to himself, "Manmohan's father has been suspended!"

Bibhuprasad remembered. that Basudev, the hotel owner, had given him a deadline. The order of his father would probably be signed today. How strange! A rock for every stone! Action and reaction … were every action and reaction of this world as balanced as this like Newton's third law of motion?

The labourer had come to Bibhuprasad by then. Bibhuprasad only stared openmouthed at him like an idiot.

He had forgotten why he had called that man to him. The man too inched closer to Bibhuprasad and stared at his face like another idiot. There was no change of expression on his face. It was a plain, detached and purposeless face. He had stared at Bibhuprasad's face with his reddish gums and the two rows of teeth hanging open.

Bibhuprasad was trying to think of a question; but no relevant question struck his mind at the time.

Suddenly, Bibhuprasad asked looking at the almost vacuous face of the man, "Do you think God is there? What's your opinion?"

There was no change of expression on the face of the labourer on hearing that irrelevant question of Bibhuprasad. Perhaps he accepted Bibhuprasad's question like any other natural phenomenon.

He only nodded his head by way of an answer.

Bibhuprasad's face had turned a bit crimson by that time. He was getting excited by some kind of inspiration and some shame or some such mixed experience. He was in a state of abstruseness and anger because of his meaningless, irrelevant question and the impertinent nodding of the head by the labourer.

The focus of Bibhuprasad's question changed suddenly. He asked again, "Why is this house being built here? Is it going to be an office?"

The labourer answered, his mouth still hanging open, "No – newspapers would be published from this place."

"Which newspaper?" This was news for Bibhuprasad. He seemed to have got a respite from the terrible experience of his first question and asked, "This looks like a factory. Is it going to be a newspaper office or a factory?"

The labourer said without much enthusiasm, "A factory – newspaper factory."

Bibhuprasad looked at the face of the labourer more closely now. He thought he had perhaps seen the man earlier somewhere; but he changed his opinion. He could understand his mistake. One did not look for similarities to identify the part of that common face which seemed to be so familiar to him. Just as one didn't look for similarities between two points in space. One didn't look for the origin of something that was the origin of everything. It could not be shaken through action. Hence, no reaction was expected from it.

Bibhuprasad's hairs stood on their ends. He trembled as if he had received some new spiritual consciousness. Bibhuprasad's eyes started shining as he looked at the hazy eyes of the man. Suddenly, he thought that the man was gradually getting inside him – like oil seeping into a wick. The man was still smiling. Those red gums looked even more reddish – exactly like the face of the vermillion-smeared Gramdevati.

That unknown thing crushed under his crossed hands on his chest had gathered so much pressure by that time that it was becoming unbearable for Bibhuprasad to take that pressure. If there was a moment when a man desired to donate all his worldly possessions without any reservation, then this was the moment. 'Vishnu woke up from His eternal sleep and created Brahma … this Creation was not there at the time … there was only a vacuum everywhere like the skies ….' A brown purse fell down in front of the man as a result of the release of pressure of his hands on his chest because of the vibration created in the process of an intimate connection between the void inside Bibhuprasad's chest and the great vacuousness on the face of the man.

Bibhuprasad picked up the purse from the ground hurriedly and extended it towards the man. Then he said in an extremely relieved voice, "I don't know if God is there or not. But look inside this and see what is there."

The man had stared the same way as before. For him, this was also a natural phenomenon. Just as the yellow leaves fell from the trees every spring, someone like this always came to him when the election came at intervals of every five years. Extending a packet towards him, he asked him, "See what is inside. Mahatma Gandhi has sent this for you."

The man didn't take the purse from his hand. But Bibhuprasad was already breathless to be rid of that responsibility.

Bibhuprasad suddenly started running after pushing the purse into the hands of the labourer as unexpectedly as he had got it.

The man was still unmoved. He opened the purse hesitantly. The smile on his face vanished all of a sudden. It was natural for him to be taken aback to come face to face with five bundles of ten rupee notes all of a sudden. He had never seen so much money in his life.

EIGHTEEN

Natabar had returned from the hospital in the meantime. As Bibhuprasad came running to the house, he found Natabar lying on the bed with his face down.

"Ho, ho! Ho, ho! The Satya Yug has arrived!" shrieked Bibhuprasad.

But there was no response from Natabar. He continued to sleep.

Bibhuprasad felt let down when he saw Natabar showing no interest in such important news.

Sukumari served tea for the two friends.

The magical hands of Sukumari again caught Bibhuprasad's attention. For some reason, that irrelevant line again came to his mind –

"Chemical Cottage Industry – that can be started without capital!"

Some time passed in this manner. Bibhuprasad went on with his monologue – about Manmohan's father. His promise to Basudev was totally forgotten. He was not at all sorry about his father. Why should he? The New Age was in the offing. The fragrance of that age had already hit Bibhuprasad's nostrils! He could find no difference today between Manmohan's father and Bhabaniprasad. Both had lost their jobs at the dawn of the new age. Let them lose their jobs! The job of one was going because of his excessive greed and that of his forefathers. The other one might also be going for the same reason – may be because of some bad deeds of the previous birth or some curse relating to that.

However, Bibhuprasad didn't have the courage to logically think further along these lines. That action-reaction or a rock for a stone theory had been creating an unknown apprehension in his mind like every other day. The fingers inside his fists cracked as on any other day.

No, no. The lack of ability to bear such a huge burden of reaction and such great heat on his ordinary hands had not been made good as yet for Bibhuprasad, the progeny of the middle class. The warning of his father chronicled in golden letters in his subconscious shined at such times to caution Bibhuprasad, "Careful! This is not your way. Reaction is not your cup of tea. Your name is 'the bounty of nature'. Look at the bearing of the earth. What does it do? It is not guided by the rule of action and reaction. Otherwise, when you sow one seed on it, it would not be turning into a green field full of grains in spite of all the atrocities perpetrated on it. You would be getting back just that one grain if it believed in reaction. It would not be returning maunds to you!"

A word or two more too beside this –

"Careful! Whatever you do – keep your hand under your control. A fountain pen looks good in this hand – not handcuffs. Vengeance is not yours …!"

The tea was getting cold. Natabar still lay quiet. Bibhuprasad had his misgivings about seeing Natabar in that state. He suddenly recalled – so, the surgery would have been performed on the old lady this morning?

Sukumari had put another cup of tea before him. Bibhuprasad looked at the tea or perhaps that Japanese tea cup. He could see the face of that apparently simple and rustic looking woman as the incarnation of Shakti as described by Natabar.

Was this the daughter of that same mother? Did she possess the same Shakti? Every helpless breath of Sukumari that he had heard the previous night hit his ears. Bibhuprasad felt as if he was dreaming a strange, impossible dream.

Bibhuprasad was quiet for a long time. Moving his eyes around the room, he observed the new order of his co-existence.

The room had become spick and span in the meantime. The boxes, the mridangam and the harmonium were no longer strewn around like the green room of a theatre party. The atmosphere of the room had changed perceptibly.

Looking at the room, Bibhuprasad recalled its history and the speciality of its name. He recalled the Gurkha. The room was under his occupation throughout the day. And it came under the control of Bibhuprasad, the researcher, during the nights. As he cleaned up the half-smoked *bidis* and shreds of paper, Bibhuprasad drew in the fragrance of jasmine flowers blooming in the neighbour's garden mixed with the cool night breeze. Bibhuprasad had initially named the house 'Niraba Malaya'! Later, it changed to 'Niraba Nilaya'.

A slight tingle ran through Bibhuprasad. He saw that Sukumari had stood nearabouts in concealment.

Natabar still lay quietly.

His inspection of the room was not yet complete. Bibhuprasad ran his eyes on the walls. The calendars hanging haphazardly from the walls still hung the same way. All those had been brought by Sukumari. Apart from the pictures of cinema stars, Radha-Krishna and Hara-Parvati in the calendars, a few needlework of Sukumari also hung from the walls – birds, trees, the sun rising on a village street, hills and an image of Gandhi.

His gaze stopped at one place as he examined all these pictures on the wall. He sat up straight and examined that particular portion of the wall.

Of course, that photograph was not the property of Sukumari. That was Bibhuprasad's property – long-forgotten, neglected and covered with cobwebs. A picture of Bhabaniprasad in his youth. Bhabaniprasad was a young man at the time. He had a forty inch chest and his neck stood straight and proud. However, something else made the picture special. Looking at the young man in the photograph, many people asked, "Did you look like this in your youth, Bibhu? Were you so handsome?"

Without being aware of it, Bibhuprasad had got up from Natabar's bed. He had walked to that particular corner of the wall and stood there. He observed the sudden change in that long-forgotten photograph. The photograph seemed to be shining brightly. A thick necklace adorned it. A speck of sandalwood paste was on the glass of the photograph. A few marks of smoke were there on the wall just below the photograph.

Shivers ran down the spine of Bibhuprasad. He felt like an image of salt getting inside the sea.

Natabar suddenly woke up. Bibhuprasad had not noticed him sitting up.

Hence, Bibhuprasad almost staggered and fell when Natabar let out an unexpected shriek. He leaned against the wall and checked the fall somehow.

"No, no, no … I'm not just a spectator … I'm Shivaji, I'm Rana Pratap! I'm Kharavela … Gangadhar Tilak … I'm Subash … friend, I'm comrade … I'm the comrade of the have-nots!" The small roof of tin started reverberating with the roar of Natabar.

Sukumari ran in.

"We've to jump into the fire … we've to save the motherland from the thieves … we've to annihilate the Thugs … we've to suffocate the Pindharis. No. I'm not only a farmer – the son of Ola Raut! I've not joined any jatra party, friend! I've joined the party of have-nots …!" The small tin roof suddenly seemed to have transformed into a huge loudspeaker.

Sukumari pulled the feverish head of Natabar onto her chest and sat down. Her face was totally guileless. As if she was used to such work.

Natabar's voice died down. The unpleasant, harsh sound gradually melted down from his wet voice. He started breathing heavily. Even then he used to shriek at intervals as if he was having a fit of hiccoughs, "I'm coming … just wait, I'm coming. They had died that day because of floods and droughts – because of the exploitations of the landlords and foreign officials. Today, they've died because of the exploitations of the 'swadeshis'. Wait – you contactors, advocates, fruit vendors, postmasters and doctors – just wait. I'm coming … I … I'm coming!"

The shrieks of Natabar were gradually dying down. He was weeping audibly by that time – on the chest of Sukumari. Sukumari was consoling him. She was telling something to Natabar the way a mother consoled a child by caressing his head when the child started retching amid the rigors caused by malaria. Bibhuprasad had been standing under that photograph like a statue.

Natabar stopped weeping after a long time. He wiped his tears and came out. Bibhuprasad followed him. Sukumari was rooted to that one place, exhausted.

Once he came out of earshot, Natabar clasped Bibhuprasad and said as if he had rehearsed the lines, "Listen! This is my final decision. You've got to take care of her. I had no illegal relationship with her ever. Now that I've stepped out to go to the battle field, I don't want any encumbrances to hold me back."

He was still in grief. He stopped for a while to get a hold of himself. Then he admitted that most dreadful event of the morning. He said, "I remembered at the last moment that surgery is not performed at an advanced stage of cancer. But the doctor wanted to pocket five hundred rupees of yours. I've thought a great deal. The surgery would have been done today. But ...."

A muscle on the thin neck of Bibhuprasad suddenly became immobile. He gripped his own neck. Natabar finished his sentence, "I gave your five hundred rupees to an election fund, Bibhuprasad."

Bibhuprasad could do nothing at the time except to stand still and be silent.

Natabar was returning towards 'Niraba Nilaya'; but he stopped when he thought of something. His dry lips were getting to be lighted by some kind of novel light.

"You haven't perhaps heard the latest news, Bibhu," he spoke from inside that silvery smile, "We've launched a united front to fight the elections. We know that our defeat is certain in this fight. We don't have money power. But do you know? We're getting Mr. Sethi to fight the election as our candidate. And you may find it hard to believe. The pregnant Murasha is still alive. Manmohan's child is still playing in her womb. She too is contesting for us. Of course, we don't need a lot of money and campaigning for her. Her belly is now her greatest asset. Capital – where one can start without any capital ... ha, ha, ha!" Natabar's face turned aside with a hazy hint.

Bibhuprasad wanted to get inside 'Niraba Nilaya' and lie down on the charpoy. Numerous needles pricked his neck. Someone seemed to be munching his fingers.

But there was no way to get back. Bibhuprasad did not have the moral courage to lock eyes with that silent image inside the house.

Natabar again returned like a storm. He vanished inside 'Niraba Nilaya' for a while. He was perhaps packing up. The election was ahead – he had to go to the villages. He had perhaps totally forgotten the old woman he had left behind in the hospital.

Sukumari came out. Bibhuprasad could not turn around to look at her. His neck had become stiff.

Extending the aluminium can towards Bibhuprasad, Sukumari turned back silently. Bibhuprasad was startled to get that silent order from her.

He had to go to the hospital. The laboratory seemed to be meaningless for him today ... irrelevant.

As he came out of the compound of 'Niraba Nilaya', Bibhuprasad turned once to look back. His eyes stopped momentarily on the small stone on which one had to put his foot before getting up on the small verandah. A lotus and two tiny feet had been drawn with the mixture of grinded rice and water. His eyes turned moist upon seeing that. He left the place as quickly as he could manage to do so.

X X X XX

After two days –

Two letters reached Bibhuprasad at the same time. The first one was a letter of invitation. Bibhu opened that first. His neck still hurt. He was again startled to see Manmohan's name in the letter.

But it was indeed the invitation to Manmohan's marriage.

Even after reading the letter of invitation several times, Bibhuprasad could not understand its real meaning. Who were that fortunate woman and her father? Bibhuprasad could not believe himself even though he read the second name several times. He had read that name so often in the headlines of important political news in the newspapers that those words seemed to be meaningless elsewhere.

Oh!! The letter of invitation fell from his hand with his deep sigh. So, Manmohan's father sold his son! So, he would be spared the suspension now! The inert doubts of Bibhuprasad were aroused again. Action – reaction; reaction – action ….

Bibhuprasad had opened the second letter in the meantime. It was his father's letter. The beginning and also the end was along the expected lines.

He had written in the beginning, "The day has finally come. I'm leaving. I have to leave. I've no objection. In a way, I feel free. Wait for the Talcher Passenger on …."

But the ending of his letter was like this –

XX X X

Who's there?

Bibhuprasad opened his eyes as he was about to doze off on the hospital verandah. It was close to dawn. He thought he heard someone's footsteps. But where?

The whistle of a train could be heard far away. The train was perhaps coming. The Talcher Passenger. His father would come back on this train. Aniruddha, his younger brother, would be returning. The results of his matriculation examination will be published in the next few days. He must be in a happy mood. He would be a college fellow in another fifteen days. Will he take science or arts?

A black bird suddenly came alive on the electric

wire stretching underneath the mango tree. It whistled indistinctly for a moment and then fell silent.

Bibhuprasad didn't open his eyes even though he heard footsteps near him again. But the footsteps stopped near him. Someone shook him and said, "Your patient is calling."

Bibhuprasad woke up. He recalled the summer vacation when he had killed a golden oriole chick with a catapult. His mother lay in the adjacent room. And his father was advising him to turn into Valmiki. Someone had pushed a bit of wet cotton into his hand and wailed, "Dear, dear! What a virtuous woman! The husband is near her. The children are around. Music is playing …."

Glossary

1 Katha Champa ..p3 ....shutter stock

2. Muchukunda .. P 3..............summer flower, pterospermum

3. Kathjodi ...... p3..............River in Odisha

4. Zemindary p 55...........small estate

5. Kirtan p 57 ....prayer in groups, singing God's various names.

6. Gur P 59...............molasses

7. I. Sc p 62.............Intermediate Science, undergraduate degree in science

8.Khudurkuni...........p 73.............................A religious festival for girls in rural Odisha

9. Bhadra ....p74.................................An autumnal month name in Indian Calander

10. Falamala ....p 74...........................Swampy areas in coastal Odisha

11. terrykhadar .....p 83.................Hand-woven cotton fabrics admixture with low percent of polythene threads

12. D.Sc. ....p 83................Doctorate degree in Science

13.Kaliyug p 87................one of the four cosmological ages according to Indian Almanac

14, Jatra, Yatra Party ....p 97...........Indian opera Party

16. Burunda ....p 97,,,,,,,,,,,,,,Name of an Opera Party

17. Kharavela ......p 98................Proper name of one of the emperors of Odisha history

18.Haldibasanta p 98......................name of an opera party

19. puranic..............p 101................mythological

20. Dal......................p101...............Lentil

21. Chuda ....p 110...............Threshed rice, serial

22. wadda..............p 119.............snack

23.Panchayat..........p 129 ....Village court for local self-government

24. khadi.............p127....................Handloom fabrics

25. Dalei Ghai ....p 131................place name where the river kathjodi had the breach in its embankment inundating substantial areas of coastal Odisha, several times in the past.

26, Mukhtiar ....p 134.............petty lawyers

27. Mridangam ....p 140..........Membrane Musical Instrument

28. Kalapahad..........p 159..............Name of a destructive Muslim general

29. Mofussil.........p176...................Rural

30. pan................p 177................chewing betel leaves

31. Brinjal.........p180....................Vegetable

32. Anna...........p182...................penny equivalent in British Indian monetary system

33. Nanka ....p184.............great famine of Odisha during British rule in AD 1866.

34. Lathi...................p 189...............stick, used as police cane

35. Homa..........p 239.................Home...............Fire place for ritualistic sacrifice of oblation, ghee, during Indian worship to gods

36. Parikud..........p239...................An island inside the Chilika Lake, Odisha

37. Atapi Batapi ....[257........Names of demon-twin

38. Shamba.........p 261...........Name of Sri Krishna's many sons as per Mahabharata

39. Shraddha ....p275.................Commemorative ceremony for ancestors

40. Gramadevati ....p 280.........Deity of Mother Goddess placed at the entry point of most Indian villages

41. Mahamrityunjaya ....p 281............Hymn of Lord Shiva for avoiding impending death to persons in dangerous situations.

42. Sunari ....p337...............Sunari in English, Cassia fistula in science

43. Mahishasura ....p 338...........Demon with a Buffalo Head, in Indian mythology

44. Rohu p 358 ....A kind of fresh water Carp fish

45. Hilsa p 358..............A kind of Hering fish

46. Mahan p 378.........A local weights and measure

47. Bidi p 378.........Local cigarette made out of tobacco rolled up in Kendu leaf

48. Swadeshi......p 381...............Products of one's own country; not imported.

Black Eagle Books

www.blackeaglebooks.org
info@blackeaglebooks.org

Black Eagle Books, an independent publisher, was founded
as a nonprofit organization in April, 2019. It is our mission
to connect and engage the Indian diaspora and the world at
large with the best of works of world literature published on
a collaborative platform, with special emphasis on
foregrounding Contemporary Classics and New Writing.